Munny - The Wheel of Life
in the Shadow of the Rainforest of Angkor Wat

FLYNN DUBOIS

MUNNY

THE WHEEL OF LIFE
IN THE SHADOW OF THE RAINFOREST OF
ANGKOR WAT

Bibliografische Information der Deutschen Nationalbibliothek
Die Deutsche Nationalbibliothek verzeichnet diese Publikation in
der Deutschen Nationalbibliografie; detaillierte bibliografische Daten
sind im Internet über http://dnb.d-nb.de abrufbar.

*Die automatisierte Analyse des Werkes, um daraus Informationen
insbesondere über Muster, Trends und Korrelationen gemäß §44b
UrhG („Text und Data Mining") zu gewinnen, ist untersagt.*

Covergrafik: irullimin / Shutterstock.com
Satz, Umschlaggestaltung und Verlag: BoD · Books on Demand
GmbH, Überseering 33, 22297 Hamburg, bod@bod.de
Druck: Libri Plureos GmbH, Friedensallee 273, 22763 Hamburg

ISBN: 978-3-8192-8816-6

CONTENTS

I. SIEM REAP

It was mid-May in Siem Reap, in north-west Cambodia. The city is famous as the gateway to the ruins of Angkor, the former seat of the Khmer kingdom from the 9th to 15th century. In its heyday, it was the size of New York City.

At this time of year Siem Reap, like the whole of northwestern Cambodia, was sweltering in the heat and high humidity. This year's rainy season was already making a violent impact very early in the year. The clouds of the southwest monsoon lay leaden over the tall tropical palmyra palms and monkeypod trees.

In the Rue Charles de Gaulle, tuk-tuks rushed past. Some undaunted tourists braved the tropical downpours and got rides to the temples. Others, already soaked from the rain, were driven in the opposite direction, back to their hotels.

Huge lakes had formed on the streets. The locals who ventured out on foot with umbrellas waded expertly through the numerous streams and pools of water in their flip-flops. Street stall owners were busy using broomsticks to make the water run off the makeshift canopies of their wooden stalls.

Kongsita, who had just dropped off the last tourist at the hotel in his tuk-tuk, was glad that he could finish a little earlier today and drive back to his family in the rainforest of the temple district. The morning had been humid and muggy, but at least there was no rain. He had brought some early risers to the entrance portal of the control points for the various temple complexes shortly before seven. He was delighted to have had, for some years past, a few regular customers who had been booking him for several days at a time whenever they came to Siem Reap. It brought him a good income.

On the Rue Charles de Gaulle, in the direction of the temple complex, the traffic gradually thinned out, owing to the unbridled downpour from the sky. In weather like this, many tourists preferred to walk through the covered markets in the city.

The intense, sweet, heavy scent of damp earth in the air mingled with the memories of a day that had been successful despite everything. He had taken some tourists to the magnificent, elaborately decorated temples and to the majestic Angkor Wat (which is even depicted on the Cambodian flag). He smiled every time at the astonished faces of the visitors who gazed in awe at the imposing structures. The thought of this historic place filled him with quiet pride.

The steady clatter of his tuk-tuk filled the humid air. The rain was now coming down harder, pelting tirelessly on the roof of his vehicle as he fought his way home. Every drop that hit the windscreen made him more aware of his great responsibility for his small family. Thoughts about this flashed wildly through his mind.

If he could put aside just a little more, his five-and-a-half-year-old daughter would be able to attend school in a year's time. This was something most people could hardly afford.

He himself had grown up without education in a family of seven children and had started work early, doing all kinds of errands for the city's shops and traders. He had been obliged to do hard physical work because he could only afford to buy a cart that he had to pull himself. Once he had his first savings, he was able to buy a kind of motorbike with a trailer. The trailer was not particularly large, as the engine would not have been able to handle a bigger load. So several trips back and forth would be necessary for larger deliveries. It was a real back-breaking job.

When he decided to buy a tuk-tuk, he had to take out an exorbitant loan from a moneylender in the city. It had been hard at the beginning, just covering the interest from his daily earnings. He had many sleepless nights, and his wife had given him a hard time at the beginning. With more experience, and thanks to tips from colleagues about where and at what times tuk-tuks were needed most, he had become increasingly established. Kongsita was very proud of what he had achieved, and he would pay off the loan at the end of this year.

He fought his way towards the checkpoint leading to the temples. The rain felt cold on his skin, even through the tattered plastic tarpaulin which barely protected him. Kongsita could hardly see the road ahead of him, but his hands steered his vehicle automatically. In the first headlights of the late afternoon, the puddles glistened on the potholed asphalt like liquid silver.

As he turned into a side street, his headlights swept across something at the side of the road. Kongsita instinctively hit the brake, causing the tuk-tuk to skid and lurch to a halt.

Through the murky view, he could just make out what looked like a small sack or bundle of clothes at the side of the road, lying in a water-filled hollow. He felt the water running down his face as he got out. The rain drummed down on him as if trying to chase him away from the place.

The bundle, which was lying on its side, had moved slightly. As he approached it, half-crouching and blinking, it whimpered feebly. The child was small, barely more than a few months old. It kicked a little. When he turned it onto its back, raindrops fell on its small, regular, fair-skinned face.

The baby looked at him out of the cloths. Large, almost astonished eyes met his. Had someone lost it? Or had it been abandoned?

He looked around. He was completely alone on the street. His thoughts raced. He had enough problems of his own. How could he possibly take care of another child?

An inner urge to leave crept over him. One step, two steps – but he couldn't go any further. The little creature's need for help stopped him in his tracks. His Buddhist conscience spoke to him. What if no one else found the child? Kongsita sighed. The decision was made before he consciously made it. He carefully picked up the child, holding it protectively against the relentless rain and waded back under the roof of his tuk-tuk.

He placed the child carefully on the driver's seat next to him. Then he gripped the wet throttle and drove off into the twilight. Kongsita sensed that this evening would change his family's life. What would his wife say?

'*Ba, Ba*!' His little daughter Sopheap threw her arms around his wet trouser legs as he entered the large family room of the hut, which was covered with palm leaves and served as both a dining and living room.

'What have you got there?' she wanted to know, her eyes wide and inquisitive.

'A baby.'

Sopheap looked at him questioningly. 'Is that how babies come into the world?'

'No, I found it by the side of the road.'

Sopheap rushed to her mother, who was just coming out of the bedroom at the back. '*Moam mi, Ba* has found a baby!'

His wife looked aghast at him and the rain-soaked bundle in his arms, a questioning look on her face. He carefully placed the baby on the large table and began to tell the story.

Incredulous, Tevi shook her head. 'But Kongsita, what are you going to do with a baby sharing the hut with us?' she asked, softly but definitely. 'How are we supposed to feed it? A baby like that needs a bottle every half hour. We can't keep the child.'

Sopheap was following her parents' conversation with great interest.

Kongsita ran his hands through his hair in desperation and snorted. 'Yes, I know, but what could I do? I couldn't just leave it and drive away.'

Tevi nodded. 'Yes, I know what you mean. Probably I would have done the same thing myself. Still, it isn't a solution.'

Kongsita let out a breath in relief, and started to answer, but he was interrupted by a plaintive whimpering cry. He and Tevi looked at each other and turned to the small bundle without saying a word.

'You see, that's what I mean.' Tevi raised her eyebrows and indicated the boy.

'I'll take the little one's wet things off for a start.' She went into the bedroom, shaking her head, and looked through the chest of drawers for some dry towels.

Sopheap bent her head over the baby. 'Does this mean I have a little brother to play with now?'

'No, sweetheart, he doesn't belong to us.'

'Then why did you bring him back with you? Is he only here on loan?'

Kongsita groaned inwardly and made a face. 'No, we are going to try to find his parents.' He said it in such a way that Sopheap knew she had better not ask any more questions. She just gave her *ba* a questioning look.

Tevi came back with the towels and wiped the baby's delicate face. 'I'll give him a quick bath, so he warms up a bit.'

Kongsita sat down wearily at the table and nodded.

When the boy was back on the table, now wrapped in dry towels, he started crying pitifully.

'He's hungry,' Tevi declared. 'I absolutely must call the midwife and ask her for baby milk.' She shook her head, looking worried. 'I would really like to know what could have driven someone to abandon a baby that was only a few months old on the side of the road in pouring rain on a day like this. Another case of poverty, I expect – with a family that already has too many children.' She sat down thoughtfully in a chair with the baby on her lap, and rocked the little one back and forth until he stopped crying. 'We should ask at the orphanage if they can take him and if they have a surrogate mother there.'

'The trip would take hours, and we don't know what would come of it. With the little ones, it can't be done,' replied Kongsita.

Tevi suddenly opened her eyes wide. 'Listen, what about Wat Damnak, that monastery with the Buddhist nun. You can drive by there tomorrow and ask if she can help us. She's always well informed and she knows a lot of people.'

Kongsita shrugged his shoulders obediently. 'Okay, I guess I can give it a try.'

The next morning, Kongsita was already sitting on his tuk-tuk at first light and driving to Wat Damnak. Damp swathes of mist were rising from last night's rain.

On arriving, he asked to see Voramay, a nun who followed the path of Mahayana Buddhism. Fortunately she had not yet left the monastery for her morning alms round.

'Sit down, Kongsita,' she said with a smile.

They sat down in the open area in front of the altar. The smoke from many incense sticks curled mystically as it diffused in the room, which was now flooded with morning light.

The nun looked at him patiently but questioningly. Her quiet dignity was impressive.

He lowered his head. 'Voramay,' he said hesitantly, 'I need your help.' His voice was no more than a whisper, but as he gave her a detailed account, he regained confidence.

'I understand.' Her voice was gentle and had a calming effect. Just from her expression, he could tell that she understood the responsibility weighing on him. Her well-proportioned face was criss-crossed with many fine wrinkles, and her alert eyes radiated an unwavering wisdom. She was probably in her seventies, though Kongsita did not know her exact age.

Voramay had fought for a long time to be recognised as a *bhik-khuni*. Becoming a fully ordained nun had been anything but easy. Despite all the resistance and hostility towards female religious, she had followed her path with conviction and was now able to pass on her Buddhist teachings and beliefs. Many, like Kongsita now, came to her regularly from the city to seek her advice.

'My wife has agreed to look after the child for now, but we can't afford it for long.' He could feel nervousness again getting the better of him.

The nun smiled and laid a hand on his arm. 'Come, let us pray for good karma and the right path for the child.' Her calm voice, murmuring the monotone mantras, sent a wave of relief through him, and gradually his tension fell away.

When she had finished, she smiled reassuringly at him again. 'I'll be going to Preah Khan temple to collect donations for the monastery and the school. I can ask around there if there is a childless couple who would like to have children. I was just about to leave anyway.'

'Voramay, I can give you a lift there. I still have to pick up a couple of tourists from their hotel in the French quarter and drop them off at the temple complex of Angkor Thom. That's on the way.'

'Thank you, I'll be happy to accept your offer.'

Kongsita quickly helped Voramay pack some water bowls and begging bowls with incense sticks and her rice snack in a bamboo cane, and then got into his tuk-tuk with her.

She smiled at him during the journey. 'You have entrusted me with an honourable task for today. I look forward to finding the right way forward for us all.'

In the late afternoon, when it was no longer so humid and the rain had eased off, Voramay planned to visit the hut of the midwife living in the jungle outside the park. She was always well informed about the latest additions to the family because, as a traditional Ayurvedic obstetrician and healer, she had access to the huts of families in the area.

When Voramay sat down in one of the central aisles of the Preah Khan temple and spread out her begging bowls, an old acquaintance joined her. It was the park ranger Nu. Voramay had known him since he started working there. They had some time for a chat every morning. He and his family regularly came to the temple festivals at Wat Damnak monastery. A small family of good people.

He was surprised that she was at the temple so early today. She told him about Kongsita's visit in the early morning.

Nu nodded sympathetically. 'I've heard the daughter of an elderly farmer at West Mebon recently lost her baby in childbirth. Shall I ask around?'

Voramay smiled. 'We'll be glad of any help you can give.'

A young girl with a rucksack in the colours of Spain on her back, accompanied by her local guide, sat down in front of Voramay and, with the help of the guide's translation, asked her for words of blessing for her future. The guide smiled a little shyly and added that he had known the girl for some years, as she kept coming back.

Voramay smiled gently and tied an orange, self-braided woollen ribbon around her wrist while uttering auspicious mantras. In return, she received a few donations from her and an open but shy smile from her big brown eyes. With perception based on experience, Voramay saw that the girl was carrying an inner grief. For a brief moment, the young woman opened her eyes wide, apparently because she felt caught out. But she regained her composure.

Voramay nodded to the guide and spoke in a quiet but insistent tone. 'Tell her that everything will work out. Nothing happens in vain, and painful feelings inside us help us to appreciate happiness all the more later.'

The man nodded uncertainly, and translated into English.

The girl looked down at her arm with the orange ribbon. A tear ran down her cheek; embarrassed, she wiped it away with the back of her hand. She exchanged a word with the guide, which Voramay didn't catch, and the two visitors said goodbye with the lotus greeting. Voramay looked after them thoughtfully.

Then a local woman in flip-flops wanted to talk to her. She asked her blessing for the planned extension to her hut.

It was now midday, and it looked as if the leaden clouds would rain down again in the next hour and into the early evening.

In view of the impending monsoon rain, Voramay decided to set off on the long journey home now and visit her friend, the midwife Kunthea, on the way.

She was in luck, as Kunthea had just come back from her first rounds when Voramay arrived. The midwife offered her a freshly prepared guava juice which Voramay found very refreshing.

Kunthea was a quite ample middle-aged woman who was held in high esteem by all the locals. Her skin was bronze-coloured, and with her smiling eyes and apple cheeks she made a warm and engaging impression.

'Are you busy with births right now?'

'No, not unduly – it's mostly young mothers who have no idea at all about breastfeeding, or who are overwhelmed by everything that comes after the birth. I'm having to give them a lot of support at the moment.'

Voramay wanted to know if Kunthea was aware of any children being lost at birth, and told her about the foundling and Kongsita.

The midwife raised her eyebrows and nodded meaningfully. 'Yes, there was a sad case the other day. The baby was too weak, probably had breathing problems. It died shortly after birth. It was a real shock for the poor girl. It was the first child, and she and her family had desperately wanted to have it. Hmmm, unfortunately there was nothing we could do. You know, it was the daughter of the farmer's wife Vanna, who has a vegetable and soup stall at West Mebon. You must know the family too.'

Voramay nodded. She had known the family for a long time, and the park ranger Nu had told her about the tragedy that morning.

'Tell me,' Voramay asked the midwife, 'do you think you could ask carefully whether this farming family could possibly take in a three-month-old boy?'

The midwife swayed her head back and forth, in some doubt. 'Well, it wouldn't be their own child. I can enquire though. I have to check on her tomorrow anyway. I'll want to go round to Kongsita's wife as well, she needs baby food for the little one.'

Voramay thanked her and looked up at the sky, a little concerned. Her old bones did not appreciate the constant dampness. She got up quickly, hoping to get back to the monastery before the next heavy rain. She thanked Kunthea for the juice and raised her hands in a lotus farewell.

She was surprised to see Kongsita in front of the midwife's hut.

He stopped his tuk-tuk next to her. 'Are you going back to the monastery?'

The nun nodded.

'Come on, get in, I'll drive you back. I've just dropped tourists off at their hotel after a sightseeing tour. Any news concerning the little one?'

'Yes, I've just spoken to the midwife. There might be a possibility for the boy. Kunthea knows a family who recently lost their newborn. She'll pop round to see them tomorrow. But don't get your hopes up just yet. Your wife may have to look after the boy at home for a day or two. If we can't find a foster family then, we'll have to report it to the authorities. Could your wife manage for a few days?'

'I think so,' he said. 'I just hope it works out with this family.'

In the early evening of the day after next, while Kongsita was still out working, Tevi received a surprise visit from the midwife in her hut.

'How is the boy doing?' Kunthea asked. 'Are you managing to look after him all right?'

Tevi swayed her head from side to side. 'I'd be quite happy if the little one got a new family somewhere soon. As Kongsita is still paying off loans and our daughter needs to go to school, we don't have much left to live on.'

'Yes, I know. That's why I asked a few families about it. The only one that really comes into consideration is that of the farmer's wife Vanna, who has the vegetable and soup stall. However, the husband turned me down yesterday. I think he and his wife are still too upset by the death of their newborn. However, they did enquire about the boy this morning.'

Tevi raised her eyebrows with interest. 'Oh, that would be so nice, almost like a twist of fate!'

She looked thoughtfully at the little one in his cot. Kunthea swayed her head back and forth. 'I completely agree with you. It's high time the little one had a family.'

Long after the midwife had left the hut, Tevi sat with the baby on her lap in front of the hut under the old knotted fig trees with their thick trunks, and tried to imagine the little one's destiny. He seemed to be a very quiet boy. Striking were his rather light-coloured complexion and his large, alert eyes which tried to take in everything in his immediate vicinity, and looked at her as if asking a question.

She went back into the hut and put the little one in his improvised bed to prepare an *amok*, a traditional curry dish, in the kitchen. She needed to have it ready before Kongsita returned from kindergarten with their daughter.

As she placed the *amok* on the dining table, she could already hear the clattering sound of the tuk-tuk. Sopheap rushed into the hut with her little rucksack on her back (she was very proud of this rucksack), and wrapped her arms around Tevi's legs.

'*Moam mi*, today I wrote words. I can write our names now! What's the baby's name?'

Tevi looked at the entering Kongsita with a long meaningful look.

'We don't know, dear,' she replied, 'he doesn't have a name yet.' She turned to Kongsita. 'The midwife brought me some more bottles of baby food today. That should be enough for the next few days.'

The next evening, just as they were finishing dinner, Tevi heard the humming sound of a motorbike turning into their mud track. Sopheap stood curiously in the open doorway. Her hand slid questioningly into Kongsita's, who was now also standing in the door.

A young couple were sitting on the machine. The man and woman politely offered a lotus salute as they dismounted.

'I am Arun, and this is Chenda, my wife. Kunthea told us that we could come round today ... er ... because of the baby.' He looked a little embarrassed.

'Do come in,' Tevi called out. She had agreed with Kunthea that the two of them could see the little one at any time. She had specially cut up some fresh fruit and arranged it on a woven banana leaf.

Tevi knew that the loss of their baby had been a hard blow for both of them. Nevertheless, after giving birth just two months ago, Chenda was a graceful young woman of twenty-two with high cheekbones and flawless skin. She wore her long dark hair up in a bun.

Arun was only three years older, and tall. Although he was very slim, almost lanky, you could see muscular upper arms under his shirt from all the lugging of goods for his parents-in-law's vegetable and soup stall. His smile was friendly but a little uncertain. Fine laugh lines had formed around his eyes.

'Kunthea told us about you... and about what happened.' Tevi got the words out with difficulty.

Arun nodded sadly, his head bowed. 'Yes, it was very difficult for us. We had actually planned to get some distance, to leave it for a while, but then Kunthea came to see my wife and told her about your baby ... er, I mean, the foundling.' Arun scratched his neck nervously. 'Please excuse our curiosity, but Kongsita, do tell us what happened. Where did you find the baby? How did it happen in the first place?'

Shyly but attentively and nodding frequently, they followed his account – shaking their heads again and again in amazement at the plight of this little creature.

While Kongsita offered them fruit and a guava juice, Tevi went to the sleeping area at the back of their hut and returned with the baby in her arms, a mischievous smile on her face. She had wrapped him in fresh white cloths.

The heads of Arun and Chenda shot up. They held their breath and tried to catch a first glimpse of the baby. The little one's big brown eyes followed what was going on around him with curiosity.

'So here is our foundling with the button eyes. Isn't he adorable?' Tevi laughed heartily.

Chenda and Arun craned their necks, each of them trying to catch a glimpse of the boy's face.

As Chenda and Arun bent over him and studied him closely, they couldn't hide their excitement. A strand of Chenda's hair had come loose and fell over the white bundle. Suddenly a small arm reached out for it, and the little one started babbling. Chenda playfully put the strand between his little fingers, and he laughed audibly for the first time. The delicate, fair-skinned face looked at her, fascinated. Almost as if he were asking a question.

Tevi smiled and winked at Kongsita. 'He really is a very beautiful boy. Just look at his eyes and his fair skin, Arun. And how strong he is, after all he's been through!' Chenda turned to Arun with enthusiasm. She looked happy.

'Chenda, could you take him for a moment? The midwife gave me a bottle of baby milk. I'll just get it.'

Chenda carefully took the baby, who was now making soft noises indicating hunger. With a smile, she rocked him lightly back and forth. Arun watched the whole scene with an incredulous expression.

Tevi came back with the bottle and handed it to Chenda. The baby began to suck on the bottle, studying Chenda intently.

'Arun, why don't you hold the baby?' Chenda smiled radiantly at him.

'No, leave it. I don't know if I would do it right,' Arun said, feeling insecure. Before he knew it, he had the wriggling child on his lap. Two arms reached out towards him.

'Maybe he wants to be held upright,' Tevi suggested. Arun placed the little one on his lap, the feet on his thighs. They looked at each other.

'I think he likes you.' Kongsita grinned mischievously.

Tevi shot Kongsita a sidelong glance in response to this rather tactless remark. But the young couple, completely under the little one's spell, didn't notice.

They were looking at one another, Chenda with an almost pleading look in her eyes.

Arun turned to Kongsita. 'The boy really is something special. I think Chenda and I will discuss it quietly this evening. We are still uncertain, and we will need to talk to our parents about it.'

Chenda looked at Arun questioningly, but said nothing, looking back down at the white bundle she was holding in her arms again. It was clear that both of them were completely taken with him.

The young couple made a grateful goodbye and left with friendly smiles. They rode the rattling motorbike back onto the road.

Kongsita had just dropped off a tourist at his hotel in the old French quarter around noon when he saw the midwife in the street.

'Hello, Kongsita, I'm just going to the West Baray reservoir to see Chenda's family. They would like to talk to you. Are you around by any chance?' Kongsita looked at his watch. He had a pickup at a hotel in the city centre in an hour. There wouldn't be enough time for him to get there and back from West Mebon. He bit his lower lip. He would have to ask a friend to fill in for him. Hopefully he would be available at this time.

A moment later, he was able to give the midwife a reassuring nod. He hoped that this was a good sign for him and his wife, as well as for the baby.

The family's vegetable and soup stand was picturesquely situated by the large water basin of West Mebon. Quite a few tourists would be milling about here. Having been on a day's mountain bike tour, they liked to get something from the soup kitchen or else just drink a cup of freshly squeezed sugar cane juice with lime.

The farmer's wife Vanna greeted him respectfully and offered him a noodle soup with lemongrass. 'This is one of our specialities,' she told him. Chenda and Arun sat down with the midwife.

'Well,' Kunthea opened the conversation, 'the families of both Chenda and Arun would like to take the little one in. I can report the birth to the authorities, they know me well. It's all right this way and it's less complicated. No one has to worry about any subsequent questions.' Kunthea nodded confidently.

Chenda's face glowed with joy and excitement. Arun gently stroked her back and smiled at her. 'We are so happy! We can't tell you how happy we are.'

The midwife smiled with satisfaction and turned to Kongsita. 'Could you give me a lift right away so that we can take the little one to his new family?'

Kongsita was swallowing the last of his soup and almost choked on hearing her words. He nodded his head enthusiastically. His wife would be overjoyed.

To celebrate this surprisingly speedy and fortunate outcome, they clinked their glasses to the big event with a freshly squeezed sugarcane juice, wishing the young couple good luck and good karma with the new addition to the family. Arun laughingly took Chenda in his arms. She had joyful tears running down her cheeks.

II. MUNNY

'Munny, please clear your school things off the table so that we can eat.' It was late afternoon and Chenda was standing in her soup kitchen, chopping lemongrass for the noodle soup on a small board. Customers were no longer expected at this time of day, and the family was usually left to itself.

The little foundling had by now grown into a lively boy of eight and a half years. They had named him Munny, which means 'intelligent' in Khmer. His large, watchful dark eyes, contrasting with the beautiful, almost elegant, light complexion of his regular features, had suggested the name to the foster-parents.

Munny more than lived up to his name. He had an amazing ability to deduce things he didn't yet know from things he was familiar with, just by applying logic. He only asked questions when he didn't understand how things fitted together. To the delight of Chenda and her mother Vanna, he was particularly interested in herbs and spices. For his age, he was already able to distinguish an astounding number of them and knew how they were used in the home and in medicine.

Voramay was responsible for the latter. She had taken him with her into the rainforest repeatedly, ever since he had been able to walk longer distances on his own. She let him feel that he was a very special gift for her and that they had a special kind of connection, almost as if she were his grandmother.

Munny's eyes lit up every time he was allowed to go exploring with her. In her own special way, gentle Voramay had become his patient mentor. Munny had idolised her since he had known her. Chenda and the whole family appreciated her attentive nature and her patience in answering Munny's many questions. She openly showed her joy and was proud, like a grandmother, that she was able to pass her knowledge on to him.

Munny had a very keen sense of smell and taste, which did not escape Arun and Chenda. He had a habit of promptly sharing this with others, which sometimes led to embarrassing situations. Recently they had been invited to a family dinner where he bluntly stated that the cook, a friend of the family, had used a spice for the curry that didn't suit.

Chenda had dismissed this with a smile, visibly embarrassed, stating that she also used it in this dish. They had only just managed to stop the vehemently protesting and recalcitrant Munny from making further inappropriate comments about their hostess's cooking.

Whenever Arun was able to take his son to the old market in town, Munny was given something to eat that he hadn't tried before. Munny liked this kind of guessing game with his father and looked forward to each new discovery. 'I must take this to Voramay and ask what can be made from it,' he would say.

Sometimes it was dried fruit or the finely ground powder of a spice or a root that inspired him. Munny always came home from the market with a new collection of ingredients, which he proudly presented to his grandmother Vanna who praised him to the skies.

Every evening, like this one, the whole family ate outside at the big table of their soup kitchen, and Munny told what he had learned at school. Without any effort on his part, Munny had become an excellent student and didn't have to study much for the assignments the teachers gave him as homework.

Munny was fidgeting at the table. '*Moam mi, Ba*, can I go to Lake Tonle Sap tomorrow? I don't have school. My friend will show me his family's vegetable fields on the water! They can walk on the water there! Please, can I go? They have chickens and a dog too.'

His parents laughed at his curiosity. Arun looked at Chenda questioningly.

Vanna laughed. 'Well, then you can see where some of our vegetables come from.'

'How are you going to get there?' Arun asked.

'Boran's father will give us a lift in his delivery truck and bring me back in the afternoon.'

Arun grinned to himself. 'You've got it all worked out, haven't you? Well, when you're finished with your chores, you can go.'

Munny jumped up ecstatically and threw his arms around Arun's neck.

Chenda laughed. 'Munny, I'll give you some rice snacks for you and Boran to take with you tomorrow. And you can take some soup from Grandmother as a gift for his family, that will be enough for all of you for lunch.' Chenda was always very careful not to be a burden to anyone. On the contrary, she was always finding small ways of showing her appreciation.

The next morning, Boran greeted him euphorically from the truck, hailing him from a distance.

Boran was a 'lad from the country', as the farmers around Lake Tonle Sap are generally known. He was very powerfully built and had a broad, winning smile. By contrast with Munny, his was an open, boisterous and impulsive character.

He was in the same class as Munny. Different as they were, they had got along well from the start and had been good for each other in their own special way. As a result, Arun's and Chenda's family had become friends with Boran's family. Boran's father supplied their soup kitchen with fresh produce from the lake. Once a week they got freshly caught fish as well.

The boys drove off, laughing jubilantly, in the back of the truck. They were obviously having a lot of fun together. Arun and Chenda waved after them. Smiling happily, she took Arun's hand.

When they arrived at Kampong Phlouk, a stilt village, Boran raced to his father's boat. 'Look, Munny, this is our boat. I can drive it already.' Boran proudly started the engine. His father came up and got into the boat, with a few tools he had brought from the land.

Munny was amazed. It was his first time at the lake. Since they lacked a means of transport and couldn't spare the money for the almost hour-long bus ride, they had never been able to afford a trip south. He enjoyed the breeze and the smells on the lake very much. It smelled a bit like when it rained in Angkor, and the earth gave off all that spicy moisture. Only now something else was in the air too: fish!

They passed the endlessly green floating fields. The lush colour reminded him of the rice fields in and around Angkor. He saw the families in their bamboo huts on stilts. Boats everywhere. It was very busy. Boats were being loaded, building materials unloaded. Nets were being repaired, plants for the fields carried on board. Steam rose constantly from cooking stoves. Munny absorbed all these impressions like a sponge.

'We're there,' Boran announced, rousing him from his thoughts. Boran jumped onto the footbridge of one of the bamboo houses and threw the line around the pole. 'Look, up there is where I live. I can see all the way to the opposite shore. Come with me, I'll show you.' He pointed to a half-open stilt house with two floors.

They raced up a steep ladder to the top floor. Munny just managed to say a hasty hello to Boran's mother on the kitchen level, before being amazed by the breathtaking view from Boran's room one floor up.

'Look, over there on the other side there's a crocodile farm belonging to a friend of ours. I often go there when *Ba* goes to his fields. I help feed the baby crocodiles. It's really exciting. Of course, they have really big ones too. The big ones are Siamese crocodiles. But they are in a big pool further away. Otherwise they would eat up the little ones.' Boran told this story excitedly, in a loud important voice.

Munny gave him a baffled look and shuddered. 'Ugh, that's really gross. I'd be afraid of being bitten by the little ones.'

'Nah, it's not dangerous. Sometimes I even take a small one out and play with it.'

Munny's eyes widened. 'Whaaat? You're not afraid?'

'No, you just have to know how to handle them.' Boran was visibly proud of his knowledge, which was met with wide eyes and an incredulous shake of the head from Munny. 'Does your *ba* know about this?' Munny asked him.

'Oh yes, of course – but I had to promise to stay away from the big animals. Besides, the owner of the farm is a friend of my parents. He buys our fish waste and the bad fish. For crocodile feed. That's how my father always gets rid of the whole catch.'

Munny let his eyes wander over the magnificent scenery. The lake was huge. He had never seen a lake that big before. His father had explained to him the night before that this was the largest inland lake in Southeast Asia. Munny couldn't really imagine how big Southeast Asia was, but this lake had to be really, really big.

'Come on, *Ba* will take us across to our vegetable fields by boat before lunch time.' Boran pulled Munny by the sleeve towards the stairs. The two of them enthusiastically dashed down and back onto the boat, where Boran's father had just loaded baskets with a few shovels and harvesting tools. When they arrived at the floating field, Boran leaped out with practised ease and moored the boat. Munny was flabbergasted. The field was like a small island. He thought that Boran would sink into the water at once. But it didn't happen. The swaying network of plant stems beneath supported him effortlessly.

'Come on, Munny. Look, you can walk quite normally here.' Boran's father helped him out of the boat, having seen the uncertainty on Munny's face. 'Look, I'm three times as heavy as you are, and it carries me. Don't worry, Munny.'

The first steps on the field felt very strange. It was almost like standing on a trampoline that was constantly moving. But then it was great fun.

'Here are some clippers. You fill the small basket with aubergines. I'll check the fish traps.' Boran's father waded to the opposite edge of the field, where he pulled a fish trap out of the water with a handful of medium-sized fish. 'These can go with your mother's soup for lunch, Munny.' Looking pleased, he tipped the small grey-brown fish into a container.

On the journey back to the hut, Munny enjoyed the refreshing wind on his face.

In the meantime, Boran's family had gathered on the first floor, the kitchen floor, for dinner. The whole family was very lively and laughed a lot. Everyone was talking at once. Three generations were gathered around the soup pot on the floor.

The grandmother was feeding Boran's four-year-old sister. Boran's mother pushed freshly fried fish pieces from the wok over to them, which everyone put into small bowls filled with a spicy fish paste. From another bowl, they spooned in the vegetable broth from Munny's mother.

Munny literally soaked up the different aromas from this kitchen. He was fascinated by how different his mother's soup tasted, even with other ingredients added to it.

Boran's mother nodded approvingly. 'Munny, tell your mother that she is an excellent cook and we thank her very much for this treat.'

In the late afternoon, Boran's father told them they must leave for the hour-long drive back. Boran nudged Munny. 'You absolutely have to come with me to the crocodile farm next time you're here. I'll show you everything. It's really exciting, and I can show you around. You'll like it.'

Munny had his doubts, but didn't want to appear a wimp and nodded eagerly.

'*Ba*, can you take us both over next time?' Boran asked his father. Busy untying the boat, he just nodded.

When they arrived home, Munny excitedly told the family all about it. 'Can I go to the crocodile farm with Boran next time? I really want to see how he feeds them. He says he has a feeding hook. Oh please, I really want to watch.' Munny was hopping from one foot to the other.

'If your marks are okay, you can go during the school holidays,' Chenda replied.

Munny couldn't get the thought out of his head that his best friend was braving the crocodiles at close quarters. He admired Boran's courage.

A week later, at school, Boran excitedly told the class how he was doing so well on the crocodile farm that he would soon be allowed to feed the larger animals under supervision. 'You know, when I finish school, I want to be a crocodile breeder too. I could feed my family with that. You earn a lot more than you do with fishing.'

Munny was speechless. He marvelled at his friend's courage and plans. He had to tell Voramay about this the next time he saw her and find out what she thought, because he highly valued her opinion and the way she looked at things.

Since he was turning nine in a few days, he knew that Voramay would come by on his birthday, which he was already looking forward to. She always brought something special with her in the way of plants and spices.

On his birthday, he ran excitedly out of the school by the monastery into the open. His father was going to pick him up today together with the tuk-tuk driver Kongsita, whose family had taken the afternoon off for him.

And sure enough, Kongsita and his wife, along with Sopheap, his *Ba* and Voramay, were all there at the school gates. He gave them all a warm welcome, and was very happy that Voramay had come with them right away.

When they arrived home, the soup stall was already steaming. It was chicken in lemongrass with lots of fresh coriander, his favourite dish.

Just as they were about to take their seats at the table in front of the soup stand, a delivery truck drove by and stopped at the side of the road, throwing up a huge cloud of dust. With much hooting, Boran got out of the truck with his father following him. What a surprise! Boran hadn't told him at school that he'd been invited as well. Munny and Boran hugged each other, laughing and slapping each other on the back. Boran and his father greeted the rest of the birthday party with friendly smiles.

'Voramay, look, this is my friend Boran. We've been at school together since the first class. Boran helps out at a nearby crocodile farm in his free time. He feeds crocodiles!'

'No, no, just the very small ones,' Boran corrected the excited Munny. Voramay looked at Boran in a friendly but searching way and nodded. 'That's not without risks, my boy. You must always be careful, and treat the animals with a great deal of respect.'

Munny felt somewhat validated by Voramay. He wouldn't have

the courage to do what Boran was doing. 'Boran plans to run a crocodile farm too when he's older,' Munny added.

Everyone looked curiously and almost questioningly at Boran's father. He shook his head. 'Well, it's certainly a lucrative business, but it's also associated with many dangers. We are not enthusiastic about these plans, but perhaps Boran will come up with other ideas in the course of time. Maybe one day he will study and earn his money in the city.'

'Yes, we hope the same for Munny,' said Chenda. 'Munny's teachers even asked us recently if we should let him skip a class, since he learns so easily and gets good marks. What do you think about that, Voramay? You know him and the things he's interested in.'

Before Voramay could say anything, Munny interrupted. 'But then I'll be in a whole new class and won't know anyone. Can Boran go to the new class too?'

Voramay nodded thoughtfully. 'Well, Munny, you would see Boran at school any time. This would be a unique opportunity for you. I think you should seriously consider it.'

Chenda and Arun smiled, obviously pleased by her words.

Boran's father nodded in approval. 'You should take advantage of this opportunity, Munny. That means one less year of school for you. Think of the time you'll save, and it's one year less of school fees for your parents.'

A bit embarrassed, Boran silently contemplated his almost empty plate.

'But I want to stay in the class with my friends,' Munny said stubbornly, pulling a face.

'Munny, you can take your time to think about it and leave it until the end of the school year,' Voramay said in her calm and collected manner, giving his parents a complicit wink. 'Look, I've brought you something from our famous library at Wat

31

Damnak for your birthday. This is for you.' She handed Munny an old-looking, slightly faded book, beautifully illustrated with herbs and plants on the front cover.

His first book!

'This is an old cookbook of traditional Khmer cuisine and tells you all about our native herbs. And it explains how to use them in the kitchen for all kinds of dishes. You can also learn how to use medicinal plants properly.' Voramay smiled at Munny's enraptured face.

His bad mood instantly lifted. He had always been passionate about this mysterious ancient Khmer knowledge that only the aged Voramay could pass on to him. He beamed and embraced her fiercely.

Chenda reminded him that Voramay was delicate, he should handle her with care. But Voramay laughed and was pleased with his enthusiastic reaction.

'Voramay, can I take it with me on our trips to the temples?'

She laughed again. 'If it's not too heavy for you, by all means! But that reminds me. Listen, you two!' Voramay looked at Munny and the still uncommonly quiet Boran. 'Would the two of you like to harvest lotus flowers and blue water lilies at the Srah Srang reservoir for our ceremony at Wat Damnak? We need them next week to celebrate the Bom Om Touk water festival. Could you two help me with that? I have some trouble with my legs getting into the water, and also some concerns about falling in where it's deep. I can't swim,' she smiled self-deprecatingly. 'I leave that to the fish.'

Everyone at the table thought it was a great idea. Munny and Boran nodded, Boran a trifle less enthusiastically.

'You could come with me after school next Wednesday. Kong-sita would give us a ride,' Voramay suggested.

Kongsita nodded, with his mouth full. Munny was pleased to

be given the task. The Srah Srang basin, dating from the tenth century, was originally only intended for the ablutions of Buddhist monks. The only exceptions allowed were for cleaning the basin, or for harvesting lotus seeds, blossoms and water plants of all kinds for temple festivals. He hoped that this way they would get to have a refreshing swim.

As a final treat, Munny's mother had made him a cake out of sweet sticky rice for his birthday. This was devoured ravenously by the boys.

After a long, relaxing afternoon, Boran's father started suggesting they should leave, as they still had a long way to go to Lake Tonle Sap and didn't want to hit the rush hour.

A few days later, Munny and Boran were standing in the water of the Srah Sang basin in shorts. They had arms full of flower stems, which Voramay gratefully received and put into baskets for the monastery. It was not all that easy to cut the tough stems of the lilies and lotus flowers, but it was a lot of fun. At least for Munny. It was perhaps less exciting for Boran than dealing with crocodiles. He stayed very quiet that day.

After a while, the nun waved her hand. 'That will do, boys, that's more than enough for our altar and the whole complex. Come, let's sit on the shore and watch the sunset.' She signalled to a woman selling fruit on the shore of the pool and ordered a large, fresh, green coconut for everyone to quench their thirst.

Just as Munny was about to make his way through the water plants to the slippery shore, he slipped and fell, gashing his shin on the ancient jagged stone steps that bordered the pool on this side.

His shin was sliced open lengthwise by the fall, and a muddy brown mess ran into the open wound. From his knee down, streams of muddy water and blood ran down his leg. Boran pulled him forcefully by the hand out of the mud. Munny made a face of pain and suppressed his tears.

He sat down next to Voramay, who immediately examined the injury with a concerned expression. 'Munny, I'm so very sorry about this. Does it hurt a lot?'

He made a dismissive gesture, trying not to look like a weakling in front of her and Boran.

Voramay took the coconut and poured the contents over his shin. 'They used this for cleaning in the past. Fresh coconut water was even used for soldiers in war when they ran out of blood infusions. It's clean and contains minerals.'

Munny followed Voramay's treatment attentively, but his face was increasingly contorted with pain. Voramay looked worried.

'Here, drink something.' She held out the coconut to Munny.

Boran watched with a serious face, eyeing the injury closely. 'We'd best get him home. His grandmother probably has some herbs that will stop the bleeding.'

Voramay nodded. She waved to Kongsita, who had parked in the shade at the other end of the water basin and had dozed off. On driving over to them, he saw Munny's leg which was still bleeding heavily and had now swollen up. 'That doesn't look good. Should I drop you off at Kunthea's so she can take care of him?'

'Good idea,' Voramay said. 'We'll ask her for some healing herbs that Chenda can brew later. She can use them to soak a bandage.'

When they arrived at Munny's house, the nun told the family what had happened and handed the plants over to Chenda. Munny's lower leg had now turned red and white and was badly swollen, and he complained of pain. Beads of sweat had formed on his forehead.

The next day Munny dragged himself to school, listless and limping. When he came home at midday he lay down, contrary to his usual habits, and fell asleep immediately. The next morning, his mother looked at his leg with great concern. It had become very swollen. They decided they had better keep Munny at home and observe him.

He had a high fever.

Boran's father came by. He was on his customer rounds and had fish for Chenda's family. He looked at the leg with a concerned expression. 'I think I'd better take you with me and drop you off at the Children's Hospital, it looks like an infection that needs immediate treatment.'

'You're right,' Arun said.

Chenda touched Arun's arm. 'Contact me immediately as soon as you know what they are going to do with him.'

Arriving at the hospital, Arun and Boran's father took Munny between them and carried him limping to Admissions. Voramay, who had come with them, offered her help, but had to realise that she must leave the boy to the doctors. Visibly distressed, with her shoulders drooping, she trotted off in the direction of the monastery.

Arun sat alone in the white-tiled hallway with worry lines on his forehead.

After what seemed like an eternity, a doctor came up and gave him a friendly lotus greeting. 'Your son has severe blood poisoning. Any later and they wouldn't have been able to admit him. He would have collapsed.'

Arun was seized by terror. Only now did he fully realise the danger Munny was in. He had completely underestimated the whole situation. He had almost lost his son! It was the first time he had found himself in such a position. He fought back tears.

'We've put him on a drip and he's getting strong antibiotics. We have to keep him here and monitor him because he's still in a critical condition. We don't yet know how long that will be, but we have to wait and see how his leg heals and how he reacts to the drugs. I'll let you know.'

'Can I come and visit him in the next few days and be with him? I'm so worried.'

'Yes, but don't come until the day after tomorrow at the earliest. By then, the fever should have gone down. There's no point before that.'

Arun swallowed, dry-mouthed. He had no idea what he was going to say to Chenda. As downcast as a beaten dog, he thanked the doctor, who patted him on the back, and left the hospital quietly. Outside the building in the darkness, his tears flowed unrestrained. He felt so helpless. He decided not to call Chenda yet, but to go home first.

Chenda covered her face with her hands in horror and cried softly. Arun took her in his arms. 'We'll go to the hospital the day after tomorrow, okay?'

She nodded on his shoulder, choked up with tears.

The next day Voramay called. 'How is Munny?'

'I'm so sorry, Voramay, I can't tell you anything about Munny's condition,' Chenda said. 'But we're allowed to visit him tomorrow for the first time. Why don't you come with us?' Chenda sensed that the nun blamed herself for having asked the boys to help her.

The next day, Chenda pushed a chair next to Munny's bed for Voramay, because she knew how much the nun was troubled by the arthritis in her legs. Chenda and Arun stood there with worried expressions. Munny's leg was bandaged.

Soon the doctor entered the room with the medical records. Without waiting for questions, he gave an initial report. 'The fever has now gone down a bit, and the inflammation in the body has clearly subsided. We have to monitor the healing process for another two days. Relapses can always occur. What worries us more at the moment is his leg. Due to the poisoning there is a lot of dead flesh there, which we have had to remove. We hope it was enough. But we can't be sure yet.'

Chenda covered her mouth with both hands in shock. 'How much longer will he sleep?'

'Well, to help him through the night, we gave him a mild sedative. That should be wearing off by now. I'll leave you alone with your boy. I'll check in on him later.' He said goodbye with a brief nod.

Voramay had meanwhile taken Munny's hand and put a bracelet made of small red sandalwood beads around his wrist. She murmured monotone mantras.

Arun and Chenda had tears running down their cheeks.

Two days later, Munny was finally responsive again and smiled wearily at his parents.

Arun smiled back at his son. 'The doctor says you're over the worst. Your leg will be fine too. They had to cut out quite a bit, but it's still good enough to play football.'

'I'm so sorry to cause you so much worry. The hospital is expensive,' Munny mused.

'Well, that's true, but at least you'll get well again. You can save us some money by moving up a class, like the teachers suggested,' Arun winked at him with a grin.

Munny nodded without smiling. Actually he took this question very seriously indeed.

'Then I must tell Boran,' said Munny, 'that he'll have to share his desk with a new classmate.'

Arun looked at him with wide eyes. 'Does that mean you'll do it?'

Munny made an effort to smile. 'Yes, I think I will. And besides, Boran and I can see each other during the school holidays. I can stay with him at the lake for a while, can't I?'

Chenda stroked her son's hand. 'As long as you're careful and look after yourself.'

Munny nodded excitedly and laughed. 'I must tell Boran right away, when I get out of here.'

When Munny saw Boran at school, Boran was not too upset about his skipping a class. 'I thought it was going to happen. In your place, I would have done the same.'

The boys met again at the lake during the next school holidays, and Munny was allowed to stay overnight at Boran's house. They spent a lot of time at the crocodile farm belonging to his parents' friend, and Boran showed him how the feeding was done.

Munny was no longer so horrified by the animals, but he still had a very healthy respect for them. His parents had drummed that into him, and he didn't want to let them down.

Boran showed him how the half-grown crocodiles were fed with fish and chicken scraps, using a pole with a pointed hook. 'Look Munny, this is how it's done. You have to pull the hook out fast enough before one of the animals rears up and bites into your hook. Then you can get it snatched out of your hand. You can look pretty stupid and lose your balance, even with a rope around your waist.'

On these forays Munny came to realise what enormous strength the animals possessed.

At the short weekends, Boran and Munny regularly went to the Srah Srang water basin at sunset to discuss 'men's stuff', as they called it. Voramay occasionally joined them, as the only 'tolerated' female. She smiled knowingly at the topics of conversation of the boys, who were now thirteen. Every now and then she gave them a tip on how some mishaps can be resolved in a simple way. Her motto was usually: 'The safest way to succeed is always to try again.'

The water basin had become their favourite place. Problems with their parents, falling in love for the first time or even an exam where they had a disappointing result – these were the matters discussed. Not infrequently in the latter case, Voramay would put in a good word for them at school. Munny's school days passed much too quickly, partly because he had more material to cover than before. The days raced by. Munny noticed increasingly that there was no longer enough time for everything. He couldn't see Boran as often anymore because his studies took up a lot of his time.

When, after a long time, he saw him again at the lake with the crocodiles, he noticed that Boran had become very muscular – and he liked to show it off. Munny on the other hand, with his delicate build, looked rather frail. As is well known, opposites attract.

'Now that I have my parents' permission, I can help out on the farm right through the school holidays, and feed the big animals too, under the supervision of our friend,' Boran said proudly.

Munny shuddered. 'Man, be careful, that is really super dangerous!'

Boran dismissed the idea. 'I've been doing it with the half-grown animals for so long now, there's not much difference between them and the adults. You have to come during the holidays and see for yourself.'

'I can't say yet whether I can come. I have the entrance exam for secondary level two just after the holidays. It's not an easy exam. I really have to study hard for it to be well prepared.'

Boran made a face and laughed. 'It would be a real shame if you couldn't come. Just for a week, what do you say, you overachiever? Could you manage that?'

'I'll try and talk to my parents. I'll have to study a lot beforehand, but I'm sure I can come for a few days.'

Boran nodded, appeased.

The school year was drawing to a close. Munny met Voramay more frequently now in the school library, since she could no longer walk long distances. She was already in her early eighties. Her laughing eyes produced more and more wrinkles in her weathered skin. She showed him around the huge book collection at the Wat Damnak monastery, singling out the ones that chimed with his interests and always urging him to borrow a few, which he took home with him.

He found that he was fascinated by traditional Khmer cuisine. Creating a dish with spices and herbs, he felt, was like painting a picture with colours that he had previously mixed himself. Only here he was creating a taste picture. Voramay warmly encouraged this talent, which was exclusively due to his extremely fine sense of smell and taste – an ability which he trained more and more just for the fun of it. It made him happy that Voramay kept giving him herbs or roots that she pretended not to know the use of. He saw through her intentions and took the opportunity to extend his knowledge.

When after all the hard work the well-deserved holidays came, and Munny arrived at the lake with Boran's father, he was unspeakably happy about the change of scenery and thankful to his parents for allowing it.

'You'll have to wait,' Boran's father told him. 'He's still busy on the farm. He's taken a holiday job there and is earning his own money for the first time. He should be back in half an hour. Our friend will drop him back from the farm. Why don't you come into the house and eat something?'

Boran's sister, Abadine, had now grown into a pretty nine-year-old. She went to the local primary school by the lake. Munny spent some time with her until he heard Boran's sonorous voice.

The two good friends hugged each other with enthusiasm.

'After lunch, shall we go further south from the village along the lake? They've opened a cinema there and there's a cool new film on.' Boran was now allowed to operate his father's boat on his own without supervision.

'*Ba* doesn't need the boat anymore today, so he's given me the keys,' he said, not without a certain pride. Triumphant at their independence, they set off.

These were fantastic and action-packed days. For Munny it was a bit like an adventure camp, as he was something of a 'landlubber', as Boran called him. Every day held a fresh surprise. Munny learned to fish with traps, to prepare fish hooks and to cook his first grilled fish. He envied Boran very much for his varied life on the lake.

The days at Lake Tonle Sap passed in a flash. As always, they visited the crocodiles regularly. Munny was amazed to see how adept his friend had become at moving around the edges of the various water basins.

'Here, you take the hook,' Boran called, pointing at a monstrous beast. 'Toss it to the crocodile over there.' Munny shook his head vehemently.

'No, I'll leave that to you. You're the specialist here.' He had too much respect.

Boran laughed uproariously. 'Oh man, you're such a wimp! Well, I just hope a coconut doesn't fall on your head in the village.' He slapped his thigh.

Munny just shrugged his shoulders with studied indifference. 'I can't do any stupid stuff and risk getting hurt, or I'll get in trouble with my parents.'

Boran nodded. 'I have to go back to school in a week too. But guess what, they want to take me on as an apprentice when I finish. Isn't that great? *Ba* has finally consented. *Moa mi* is still quite cross with me. She doesn't want me to do it, it's too dangerous and all that.' He beamed from ear to ear.

The following Sunday, the two friends said goodbye.

'See you in a week at school,' Boran said, hugging Munny. He gave him a hearty slap on the back.

'Okay, don't let them eat you. They don't like you, after all, they prefer chicken.' Munny grinned.

He was actually sorry to leave the idyllic landscape.

But he still had a hard week of learning ahead of him, and the exam was scheduled for the Monday after next.

Ten days later, he had the results in his pocket. He walked home beaming with joy and proudly showing off the exam report. He just had to tell everyone about his huge success. They'll be so excited, he thought. He was already over the moon at the thought of seeing their stunned faces.

As he ran up, sweaty and with the certificates in his hand, he recognised Boran's father's delivery van in front of the soup stand. Boran must have come to surprise him! He couldn't wait to tell him how the exam had gone.

Strangely enough, he didn't see him anywhere. Everyone was probably sitting inside the soup kitchen. That was peculiar, especially with the glorious sunshine. He felt uneasy.

When he entered, he saw his mother's tear-stained face, and Boran's father was also staring at the floor, his expression stony.

'Ah, Munny, come in.'

42

Munny looked questioningly at his father, whose face wore a serious expression.

'Munny, there is some very bad news. Come, sit down.'

Munny's eagerness to tell them about the successful exam was gone. An unpleasant tension got hold of him. Slowly, almost tentatively, he sat down.

'Ravi has just told us that his son went to the farm one last time on Sunday morning before school started again.' Arun spoke haltingly, his voice choked with tears. 'He wanted to give the animals their morning feed.' His father heaved a heavy sigh. 'Munny, a terrible, incomprehensible tragedy has occurred.'

Boran's father sobbed with deep anguish.

'One of the big crocodiles got hold of the hook he was holding. He hadn't pulled it back quickly enough. Boran lost his balance on the edge of the pool and fell into the water with the crocodiles.'

Shivers ran down Munny's spine. His scalp tingled like crazy.

'The crocodile farmer heard a scream and ran to the pool.' Arun swallowed desperately. 'He was able to pull Boran out by the line that was around him, but even those few seconds were too long.' Arun's voice trembled. He tried hard to be strong and suppressed his tears with an anguished face.

Boran's father had buried his face in his hands, expressionless, and Chenda too was covering her face with her hands and weeping.

Struggling not to break down, Arun took up the story again. 'Boran was unconscious from the pain. But it was too late. The crocodiles had inflicted very serious bite wounds all over his body and severed the main artery in his arm.'

Ravi sat apathetically on a stool, staring at the brown clay floor. Munny looked from one to the other, his eyes wide open. 'How is he? Where is he now? I want to see him.'

His father struggled for words. 'He bled to death on the way to the clinic. It was too late to help.' Arun could no longer control himself and wept.

Tears welled up in Munny's eyes, and he gasped for air, jumping to his feet in shock. He was completely bewildered, as if the ground had been pulled out from under his feet. Anger and sadness were written all over his face. 'Is he?' Munny screamed from the deepest part of his soul. 'Dead?'

Arun nodded without looking at him.

Blind with tears, Munny shot out of the soup kitchen and into the open, knocking over a chair. Where should he go? He felt so incredibly helpless and small. He had to get out of there. He started running.

Of all people, it had to be Boran – Boran, who literally could not be unsettled by anything! He ran aimlessly along the eastern Baray towards the temple grounds. He had no idea where to go. When he finally sank down on an old pile of stones in the temple ruins, breathless and with a tear-stained face, he let out a miserable howl.

He had lost a friend. He felt as if he were in a terrible dream and trying to fight his way out, but kept being drawn back into it again. He shook himself desperately and secretly hoped that it was all a big mistake. Never before in his short life had he felt such a sharp inner pain.

From behind, the sound of a tuk-tuk approached. It drove past him, stopping a few metres further on.

It was Kongsita, who got down and approached him. 'Munny, my goodness, you look terrible, whatever has happened?'

'Kongsita, can you take me to the temple?' he wailed, sniffling pathetically. He wanted to be with Voramay now.

'Don't worry, I'll take you. Come, sit in front and tell me all about it.'

Munny told him what had happened, brokenly and with agitation. Kongsita was visibly shocked and shook his head in disbelief again and again. He kept his arm around Munny's shoulder for the duration of the drive.

When they arrived at the temple, Munny charged into the entrance, distraught. Still beside himself, he forgot to thank Kongsita.

In a side corridor he found Voramay sitting in the shade, talking to one of the temple guards.

He fell weeping on her neck. Actually this was in breach of the rules – you weren't supposed to hug a nun. Voramay patted him sympathetically on the back and looked deep into his face with a calm, deliberate gaze. His voice cracked as he told her about Boran.

She nodded wordlessly, with a seriously composed expression on her face. 'You know, Munny, in Buddhism we have the doctrine of the four noble truths. They help us to process pain. We all have to learn this sooner or later.'

'But he's dead now, and it isn't fair,' Munny blustered angrily.

'Look at it this way: we are all caught in a cycle of existence, of death and rebirth, what we call samsara. The cause of this is karma. This doctrine is supposed to help us understand and cope with life.'

Munny sat by her with vacant eyes.

'You have to learn to give up Boran as a person in your imagination. But it is still quite difficult for you to recognise this now and to see beyond the pain.'

Her soft, gentle voice had a calming effect and her words took on a power, almost a magic, that he could not resist. His thoughts, however, raced and his tears did not stop flowing. He was desperate because her words and her advice made no sense to him.

How could he forget Boran as a person? He would never do

that! He wanted to ask Voramay so many things, but he had a lump in his throat and was unable to put his pain and anger into words.

The old woman stroked his back sympathetically, giving him a gentle look. 'Munny, something like this is a long process. Our inner selves heal only slowly. But if you try to recognise and understand the eternal wheel of life, what we teach, it will get better and better.'

Her calm voice got under his skin, it felt as if she was caressing his very soul. He nodded once or twice, accepting fate. But understanding? No! When would he ever understand?

'Munny ...' Voramay looked him straight in the face, which was completely wet with tears and covered with muddy rivulets ... 'Munny, I have an idea. How about we pray for Boran? For good karma? Our positive thoughts, words and actions should continue to work for him in the future. We can do that together with Boran's parents and yours.'

Munny nodded sadly. What other choice did he have?

'I'll talk to your families. But now we'd better go home. Your parents will be worried about you.'

III. APPRENTICESHIP YEARS

The next three years of secondary school at Wat Damnak passed extremely quickly. They were packed with lots of new knowledge and experiences for Munny.

Meeting him in the monastery's library, Voramay had often asked him about his interests recently. He could tell from her knowing eyes that she had something in mind. He was now seventeen years old and was certainly keen to share his knowledge of medicinal herbs, spices and Khmer cuisine, but didn't know how.

He had become a tall, very good-looking young man, with high cheekbones and bronze-coloured, but still quite fair skin. His slightly slanted dark brown eyes gave his face a rather mystical, mysterious look. His appearance evidently met with approval – from his female classmates, who invited him on a wide variety of occasions.

There was a pretty schoolmate of his, Nicole. She was the daughter of a French couple who had built up a big furniture business. Nicole adored him, focusing on him with her blue-green eyes. 'Munny, we're having a barbecue in our garden. Will you come?' Or she would say: 'Munny, my friends and I are going to the cinema. Won't you come with us?'

Munny couldn't avoid her offers. But they embarrassed him, and he almost always turned down her invitations. He only accepted if a friend would accompany him. He enjoyed being idolised, but was always aware that there was a world of difference between him and the girls. Since he was not in a committed relationship with Nicole, this only made him more desirable in the eyes of the other girls. He was friendly but cautious, and elegantly avoided any advances.

Voramay was friends with Paul Wallimann, a Swiss chef and food engineer by training, who had come to Siem Reap years ago because of his love for the place. He was apparently a very well-known star chef from near Zurich, for whom the hustle and bustle of the hotel business and the pressure to constantly reinvent himself and to live up to star cuisine standards had become too much. Since he had settled in the village, he and his partner had dedicated themselves to training children from poor, large families in the restaurant business. As a small contribution to this cause, guests paid a little extra for their meals. This financed his school, the students' accommodation and the many garden complexes from which the needs of the restaurant were supplied.

Voramay regularly recommended to him children from the school who she thought would be suitable and would be well looked after there. Paul's project was a non-profit project. His aim was to get the children off the streets.

The hotels were now queuing up for graduates of his cooking class. They were in particular demand in the service sector, for which they were trained at his school.

Based on Voramay's description of Munny, Paul and his partner Sara were enthusiastic and curious about the young man with his special abilities.

Munny was a calm and level-headed half-grown adult. Boran's death had left a deep impression on him and made him reflective. He now recognised life and death as being on the same plane, and understood better what his patient mentor had told him back then.

Paul invited Munny to do a test cook at his restaurant. He asked him a lot of questions about the ingredients of Khmer cuisine, and was very much surprised at his excellent knowledge.

When he was unsure, Munny's amazing sense of smell helped him out. Most of the time, he was able to determine which dish the ingredient was used in.

'You have great potential,' Paul told him. 'I'm happy to help develop your career.'

Since Munny lived quite close to the training centre, he didn't need accommodation there and was able to return home every day.

Paul and Sara were calm and reflective people. Paul was a powerful, wiry man in his mid-fifties. He kept pushing his thick-rimmed black glasses up on his head when he talked. His short, dark hair was already showing the first signs of greying. Sara, who was also of athletic build, with her large, brown-green eyes and blonde, shoulder-length hair, seemed like the calm counterpart to the lively Paul.

Munny liked the couple's friendly, affectionate manner. But he was extremely surprised to see the curriculum. It included business knowledge and natural sciences as well as service, kitchen lessons and organisation.

Over time, Munny created more and more imaginative dishes. He showed enormous creativity and was encouraged by an enthusiastic Paul to do even more.

The restaurant's growing success and the creations that he arranged so delicately on the plates gave Munny a certain sense of validation. Paul decided to introduce him to nouvelle cuisine.

Crispy, lightly fried vegetable pieces, served with or without meat, now enriched the menu at the Haven restaurant. Well-known culinary platforms praised the restaurant project and its creative compositions. Munny was very proud of his first small successes. Salads, lukewarm or cold, enriched the selection of starters. He always tried to create well-balanced menus. The evening booking rates were overwhelming. Reservations were now being taken up to two weeks in advance. There was no chance of getting a quiet table in the garden at shorter notice.

Munny's marks in the cookery school were excellent. At the beginning he had some problems with the commercial calculation.

'You need to know this is essential for hotels, so they don't over-order food or even order the wrong things. Food is a very perishable item, after all. What is more, every single dish has to be affordable for the restaurant and must have a margin. That makes up the profit, from which, among other things, all the staff have to be paid.' Paul looked at him, nodding gravely. 'Please remember what kind of kitchen you're cooking in. Otherwise, you won't make any friends.' He pushed his glasses up to his hairline to emphasise his meaning.

This explanation made sense to Munny. Paul had also shown him how many families would be fed from the leftovers if too much food were ordered. The numbers were incredible.

After his first year of training was completed, Paul stuck his head in the door and looked at him seriously. 'Munny, could you come with me to the office.'

Munny was already feeling uneasy and wondering what he could have done wrong. But Paul and Sara smiled at him when the three of them stood in the boss's office.

'Here are your new work clothes.' Paul handed him a completely black outfit with gold-embellished buttons, bearing the restaurant's name and his own name on the top right. 'As you know, students at our restaurant only receive these chef's jackets for special skills in their third year of training. But you are already so far ahead of the others that we have decided to give you this in recognition of your achievements so far.'

Munny looked at the two of them in disbelief. They laughed at his bewildered expression. 'Come, try it on so we can see if it fits and how you look in it.'

Munny beamed with pride and had donned his new black outfit in no time.

'Wonderful!' Paul commented drily. 'From now on, you can tell the others how they can help you. As of now, you're only responsible for the menu and new creations. And of course for the organisation. Like a sous-chef in a big restaurant.' Paul gave Munny a complicit wink.

Munny was on cloud nine. Voramay and his parents would be amazed at his progress. After the lunch break, he happily ran over to Voramay and told her about his promotion.

She beamed and patted his hand. 'See, your good karma is coming back to you. You have done very well.'

'Voramay, will you come to my parents' house for lunch?'

She shook her head. 'No, I'm not walking well today, and I'm tired too. Another time.' She was now in her late eighties and had become frail in recent years. Munny was concerned to see how much she had changed.

At home, the joy at his success was overwhelming. Arun disappeared briefly into one of the back rooms and came back with a small, cloth-decorated box. 'Look, Munny, we and your grandmother have saved up a very decent sum of money for you. We've seen how hard you've worked for your success and we're incredibly proud of you. You give us unspeakable joy. The money is to be your first starting capital for your new profession, wherever you choose to work.'

The whole family stood around him. Munny swallowed,

dry-mouthed, with a lump in his throat. He knew how hard his family had to save to put something aside. Tears of emotion welled up in his eyes. With a faltering voice and an incredulous shake of the head, he managed to stammer out his heartfelt thanks. 'Thank you – thank you so much.'

The next two years were marked by experiments and new experiences in nouvelle cuisine for Munny, especially since he had discovered that this style of cooking was very well received by the guests. Something was perhaps also due to the spirit of the times, with its inclination to a healthier diet. Paul's kitchen had gladly adopted this style, especially since it had established itself everywhere in the world of haute cuisine.

'Paul has told me he'll try to get you a kitchen job here in Siem Reap at the Raffles Grand Hotel,' Arun said cautiously as Munny sat at the table one evening. 'They value his opinion there. It's probably not a big deal for you, since you'll be starting at the bottom, but you'll just have to persevere. Of course there's a lot of competition because everyone wants the job.'

Munny could already see himself coming and going at the time-honoured Raffles Hotel. It would be a great opportunity for him, if he were so lucky. With its imposing façade and tall Palmyra palms and bougainvillea to the front of it, the plantation-style hotel in the green old town of Siem Reap, within sight of the Royal Palace, was a highly elegant French Art Deco relic from the 1930s. Film greats such as Charlie Chaplin had appeared there. It would be a tremendous honour for him to be taken on.

His last year of training with Paul and Sara was coming to an end. Munny almost regretted it. The two of them with their cooking class had become something of a second family for him.

A week before the end of the training year, Paul called Munny into his office with a mysterious air.

He rose solemnly from behind his desk. 'Munny, I have something for you.' He smiled mischievously and took out a black box from his drawer. 'Do you know what this could be?'

When he opened it, Munny saw a black velvet cloth with several items wrapped in it. 'This is something special. It was given to me back in the day when I left Switzerland. Now it belongs to you.' Munny made a surprised face and lifted the black cloth. A box came into view. Before him lay a mysteriously gleaming and very exclusive collection of five knives.

His jaw dropped open, and his eyes moved back and forth between Paul and the knives.

'This is your starter set of knives. They're three-layer Japanese Damascus steel.'

He knew the inestimable value of these knives from his training. 'My goodness ... I can't accept this,' he stammered.

'Yes, you can, it's okay. You've been very ambitious and hardworking. That deserves to be rewarded.'

Munny was speechless at this accolade, and stood before Paul looking lost and awkward. He had no words.

Paul regarded the stunned young man with a grin, gave him a big hug and patted him on the back. 'You've earned it. Now take good care of the knives! They're very rare.'

Munny nodded, deeply moved, and shook his head. This was his most valuable present so far. How he would have liked to tell Boran about it! His friend would certainly have been thrilled by the knives.

'Oh, by the way, Munny, I've received a positive response for you from the chef and management of the Raffles Hotel.'

Munny cheered inwardly. This is what he had always wanted. A dream come true!

'You can start there in three weeks. It's a sad day for us, as we would have liked to keep you. But there it is: I know that a young person like you wants to prove himself. Your salary there is the lowest starting rate in the kitchen. You have to show what you can do and work your way up. It's no picnic.' Paul looked at him seriously over the rim of his glasses. 'But don't let it throw you. Be patient. One of the chefs, a friend of mine, will keep an eye on you.' Paul winked at him.

Munny's heart beat faster. He had managed to get into one of the most sought-after and highly rated hotels!

'If they think you're suitable there, they might recommend you to other sister hotels in the chain. That way, you could see the world too.' The prospect gave Munny goosebumps. He had never been out of Cambodia!

Munny burst into the monastery unannounced late that afternoon. 'Voramay! Guess what? I've got a job at Raffles, the old hotel just round the corner from you!'

The nun smiled lovingly at Munny, and stroked his shoulder with appreciation. 'You see, your efforts have paid off. You have good karma.'

For some time, he had noticed that Voramay was less often to be seen in the temple grounds. The arthritis that had now affected most of her joints made her slower and more awkward. She was always getting Ayurvedic herbs for teas and ointments from a healer, but this did not really bring about the desired improvement. She categorically rejected conventional medicine. She bore the pain like a task to be overcome, in accordance with her Buddhist teachings.

Munny, who had bought a bicycle with his first earnings, rode to his parents' home, carrying his new prized possession, the knives. What would they say to that? He threw his bike down next to the canvas-covered dwelling and burst euphorically into the soup kitchen. Vanna, his grandmother, was often to be found at the soup stand at lunchtime. A group of cycle tourists with their guide had just sat down and were visibly enjoying themselves.

Munny's mother was busy chopping ingredients. When she looked up, she saw the sparkle in Munny's eyes and put the knife down. 'You look happy. A successful day at the restaurant?'

Munny couldn't get the words out fast enough. 'Guess what? I got the job at Raffles.'

Chenda was speechless.

'Remember how we used to stand in front of that huge white building, and always dreamed about going in for a drink?' Munny asked.

Chenda nodded thoughtfully. 'Yes, but it was out of reach for us, we could never afford it. My goodness, Munny, I'm so happy for you!'

'And look, Paul gave me these knives. They're real Damascus steel. Worth a fortune.' He pulled the box out from behind his back.

Chenda covered her face with her hands in amazement.

Munny looked proudly at his mother. 'Paul was given these by his boss when he left his last job, and now he's given them to me.'

'My goodness, that's very generous of him,' Arun, who had just returned from work, nodded appreciatively.

'We are so immensely proud of you.'

Munny swelled with pride. 'When I start at the hotel, you can come and visit me and see where I work.'

'Munny, I think you're getting carried away. We are very simple people, they would never let us into the hotel.'

'We'll have to see about that,' said Munny stoically.

IV. RAFFLES GRAND HOTEL

When Munny rang the bell at the side entrance of the hotel on his first day of work, a short, rather stocky man opened the door. He was wearing reading glasses perched on the tip of his nose, and a white chef's jacket with ball buttons bearing the logo of the hotel.

Munny quickly introduced himself. The man nodded wordlessly and led him into the building. Munny looked around. He hadn't expected the staff quarters to be so basic. He followed the man in silence to a room where he received his work clothes.

'Here's a locker for your things. I'll wait for you outside. Call me when you're ready. And please put this plastic cap on. We don't tolerate any hair in the kitchen.' Before leaving, he turned around. 'Oh, by the way, my name is Finn.'

Munny nodded rather shyly. When Finn, who was evidently the sous-chef, introduced him to the others, most of them murmured a brief greeting. Some of them only looked up momentarily. Others just continued chopping.

Finn turned to Luan, a Thai chef. 'Please show Munny how he can help you.' Luan nodded and led him to a large cutting board with bowls for different types of vegetables. 'We cut them this size.' He pointed to bowls of already chopped vegetables. Munny nodded and eagerly set to work.

'When you've finished that, Luan will tell you what to do next. We're currently preparing the lunch menu for our full-board guests. All preparations must be completed by eleven o'clock.'

The sous-chef gave him a rather stern look over the rim of his reading glasses.

Munny was a fast learner. But somehow he had imagined it all differently. The sous-chef was Paul's friend, but you wouldn't have known it.

On the whole, everyone in the kitchen worked ambitiously and at a fast pace, but Munny found the atmosphere impersonal. And he was a little surprised at first by the blunt way colleagues spoke to one another.

It was an international team, but there was rarely any sign of warmth or liveliness. Munny thought to himself, feeling glum, that his colleagues were probably not familiar with the principles of respect and attentiveness. He sensed that he couldn't afford to make any mistakes. It was as Paul had told him: there was a certain pecking order. Praise was rarely the order of the day. It was different from what he had been used to with Paul. Colleagues' mistakes even got reported to the management. Not much team spirit there, thought Munny.

Months later, Munny had settled into the work routine, but he was beginning to get bored with the monotonous work. As far as he was concerned, it just consisted in chopping all kinds of ingredients and spices.

When he expressed his frustration to Voramay, she reminded him that patience is a virtue that comes from a strong spiritual base. 'You see, Munny, patience is an inner strength. You are still young and want to reach your goal quickly. Think of this as an exercise for you.'

Munny wanted to protest at Voramay's words, but felt that she was right. He was just so disappointed that his skills went unnoticed. He decided to wait another month and then ask Finn carefully what other tasks he had for him in the kitchen. He was so eager to create dishes and show the variety he was already capable of. Even if it were only starters.

He kept on chopping patiently, over and over. When he wasn't chopping anything, he was responsible for the kitchen cleaning service, especially after everyone had left their workstations. He wiped the floors, the stoves and the work platforms, and couldn't suppress his frustration. A semi-skilled Cambodian kitchen boy, Dang, perhaps a good year younger than him, helped him with this task.

'What's bugging you?' he asked Munny with a grin.

'Oh, this work is so tedious. I've been a kitchen boy here for months. Nobody wants to know about my cooking skills. I was able to gain more experience at my last job. This one's no fun at all.'

Dang nodded in agreement. 'Yes, I understand. But they do that to everyone who starts here. The last one left after just three months to work at a new hotel on the motorway.'

Munny looked up, cloth in hand. 'Who can I talk to about something like this? Would it be worth talking to Finn? What do you think of him, anyway? He's a friend of the guy who trained me, but to be honest, he hasn't really shown much interest in me so far.'

Dang shook his head. 'You know he always has too much on his plate. Try his office in the staff quarters on the floor above. He's always there after the lunch guests have left. That's when he puts together the evening's menu. Maybe you'll have better luck if you catch him then.'

'Thank you, Dang, that's very kind of you. Tell me, what exactly did you get hired as?'

'Well, I'm what you might call a dogsbody.' Dang grinned across his broad, childlike face and shrugged his shoulders. He didn't seem to have a problem with it.

After a day of pondering, Munny decided to seek Finn out in his office. His heart was beating up to his throat with excitement.

He swallowed with a dry mouth as he knocked on the door. Not hearing anything, he knocked a little harder.

When Finn opened the door, he grinned at Munny in surprise. 'Munny, to what do I owe the honour?'

Over his shoulder, Munny glimpsed a sheet of paper on the desk and nodded in appreciation. Finn had his desk in a beautiful, brightly lit room with a view of the hotel garden.

'Come in and take a seat,' Finn said. 'Look, I'm sitting here with tonight's menu and tomorrow night's menu. I still have to discuss this with our chef de cuisine, Luc. We have a larger party tomorrow, so we have to organise the dishes differently.'

Finn studied him. 'Tell me, what can I do for you? Paul told me that you are well versed in Khmer cuisine.'

'Yes ... er ... I like it a lot.' Munny scratched the back of his head in embarrassment. 'Actually, I wanted to ask if I could cook something sometime, or just create a few appetisers. The work I've been doing for the last three months is very – well – monotonous.'

Finn nodded and looked thoughtfully out over the garden. 'Hm, there might be a job for you for the rest of this week. Tao Bang, who is responsible for the hors d'oeuvres, has called in sick. You could apply your knowledge of Khmer cuisine to the starters. But I'll have to check with Luc first. He's French, you know, and very particular when it comes to organising his kitchen.'

Finn dialled a number on his phone.

Munny was inwardly jubilant, hoping that he would soon be able to show his skills. He looked again at Finn's draft menu while the other was on the phone. He noticed that the foie gras that Finn had proposed would go very well with the native morning glory, a type of water spinach that is served crisp and lukewarm, along with fresh Kampot pepper.

As he tried to picture everything in his mind's eye, Finn, who had just put down the receiver, pulled him out of his thoughts.

'So, you've got the job starting tonight. Don't disappoint me. I put in a few words of praise for you with our French boss,' Finn grinned.

Munny beamed at him and nodded excitedly. He stood there wordlessly, unsure whether to make a suggestion.

Finn turned his head to the side, without taking his eyes off Munny. 'Something you want to say?'

Munny cleared his throat. 'I once served foie gras with a lukewarm morning glory out of the wok as a side dish, along with lightly sweetened tamarind mousse and fresh green pepper.'

Finn raised his eyebrows and scratched the back of his head thoughtfully. He looked at his own draft again, then back at Munny, visibly surprised by his idea. 'Yes, you're right, that's not half bad. Something of a French-Cambodian fusion suggestion about it.' He nodded appreciatively at Munny. 'So, then, get three suggestions for today and tomorrow night down on paper, and bring them to me by four o'clock. But make sure that we have all the ingredients in stock first.'

Munny went out, pleased that he had been so assertive. Now feeling highly motivated, he sat down in the spotless empty kitchen in front of a blank sheet of paper.

He thought of the book about ancient Khmer cuisine that Voramay had given him. The art was to combine a few spices with the right local vegetables or salad, and to add a light, spicy or sweet dressing.

He came up with dish that consisted only of small local aubergines in a spicy kaffir lime sauce, to be served on a banana leaf with banana flowers.

His second idea was based on the traditional beef dish *lok lak*. This is a finely chopped beef salad in a fish sauce, along with a root similar to ginger, which is used to make a syrup. This galanga root gives a slightly sweet flavour. The whole thing is garnished with kaffir leaves and coriander.

His third dish was aimed at fish lovers. It was to be a green mango salad mixed with smoked fish and small pieces of pomelo fruit. Munny added a few ingredients here and there or changed a garnish. As with Finn's drafts, he gave a list of the sauces, marinades and spices so that the work steps could easily be organised.

He looked at his watch with satisfaction after an hour. Should he present his suggestions to Finn now? He decided to wait until shortly before four o'clock.

He was looking forward to telling his family about his first success.

At half past three, Finn came into the kitchen. 'Ready already? Let me see!' Finn studied the suggestions carefully and laughed. 'Well, our accounting department will be happy. There's a big profit margin in your suggestions. No, seriously: the suggestions are great. They show local cookery at nouvelle cuisine level. I think Luc will like that. You really do have a lot of potential. We'll see where else we can use you. You choose two people to help you out and get this ready. We'll do the same tomorrow, so you'll have practice in how to realise the dishes for the gala party, which will be twice as big. The numbers are still to come. So don't just stand there, get on with it!' Finn hurried out without saying goodbye, still caught up with his thoughts.

Since it was no longer worth going home, Munny decided to visit Wat Damnak as it was nearby, and seek out Voramay. She smiled at him and nodded meaningfully. 'I'm sure you'll be good at whatever you do, since you do it with passion and conviction. Listen, you remember the green coconut juice that I poured over your injured shin? Why don't you make a soup out of the fresh juice? It always tastes slightly of lemon. You could do something with that, couldn't you, or maybe a sweet jelly?'

Munny's imagination went over Voramay's idea, and he decided to act on it at the next opportunity. It was always nice to see how much the lovable elderly nun encouraged him to try out new things.

Happy and feeling enthused, he returned to the kitchen. Dang was already there, waiting for him.

'Dang, there's news.' Munny stood proudly in front of him. 'We're getting our first big job!'

Dang clapped his hands in delight. 'You see, it wasn't that hard.'

'Listen, Dang, I'm allowed to appoint two people here in the kitchen to prepare these starters. Would you like to work with me?'

Dang nodded enthusiastically.

'Who else could we add to the team? The Chinese boy?'

'Nah, he's assigned to the pastry chef,' said Dang. 'But there's still the apprentice from southern Europe in his last year of training.'

Munny shook his head. 'I took a look at him once. He's not so keen on working, and he's also very slow and somehow un-motivated.'

'Yes, you're right about that. I don't think they'll be taking him on anyway. People have to work their socks off here for relatively little money. But we could use him to chop vegetables. I'll arrange the plates according to your specifications and you do the frying in the wok, the garnish and the final preparation of the dishes. All subject to your final approval, of course.' Despite his menial role, Dang had learned a lot by keeping his eyes open.

Munny was pleasantly surprised and grateful for his experience. 'Come on, let's get started together before the others arrive. I don't want to miss any tricks on my first assignment today. This just has to work.'

Dang nodded at Munny, beaming. 'Sure, we can do this!'

When the other kitchen staff and chefs, including Luc, arrived, the two had already pre-cut and prepared a considerable amount. They assigned the European apprentice to continue slicing. Everything went like clockwork. The plates were in the preparation stage, the cold dishes almost ready, but still without dressing.

When the restaurant manager gave the go-ahead for the starters, Munny quickly stir-fried the vegetables and beef before garnishing the plates. The garnished cold mango salads were placed on the counter for collection by the waiters. The apprentice was responsible for delivering the salads that had already been prepared. Everything was going fine so far.

All the starters were almost ready and about to be served when Munny suddenly realised that he was missing the remaining salads that had not yet been dressed with his special lime dressing. The row of twenty was missing. He looked around in panic. 'Where did you put the remaining salads that were not yet ready?' he asked the apprentice, his voice rising.

'I put them over there,' he replied, visibly bored, pointing to the pick-up counter.

'But those are the finished starters. I specifically told you that,' Munny snapped at him angrily.

The apprentice just shrugged. 'Well, they've already gone then.'

Munny clenched his fists – for the first time in his life, he really felt rage welling up inside him. 'You idiot!' he shouted at him.

Before he could yell at the apprentice any further, Dang pulled him by the sleeve. 'Come on, we still have some left over, we can just make a few more.'

They prepared the salads in no time at all. Unfortunately, the first salads soon came back to the kitchen almost untouched.

'Who prepared these?' asked the head waiter with a look of reproach. 'They're completely bland, ungarnished and without dressing. The guests sent them back. Who screwed up this time?'

Munny hung his head. 'The apprentice accidentally put the salads on the wrong side. We already have a few new ones here. Sorry.'

'Oh, the apprentice, is it! You're responsible for the apprentice, got it? If he messes up, it's your fault. Remember that!'

Munny just nodded meekly, and the head waiter swept out of the room carrying the new salads in both hands.

The apprentice shrugged his shoulders in a blasé manner.

'I'm not having you on my team ever again,' said Munny, but the other just responded with a twisted smile.

Munny was still seething. He had wanted to prove himself, and now this idiot had messed everything up for him. He saw that his boss Luc, who had been working silently hitherto, had followed the whole thing out of the corner of his eye, notwithstanding his own hectic job, with raised eyebrows. Munny was glad that he didn't scold him in front of everyone like the head waiter. Perhaps that was still to come.

'Well, you know,' the apprentice said, 'when I'm done here, I just go back to my parents' hotel. It doesn't concern me anymore.'

Munny glared as he confronted him. 'Hoorah, then we're rid of you – you loser!'

What he had learned from Voramay actually forbade him such outbursts, but today he just felt like it.

Dang touched his shoulder from behind. 'Come on, the first empty plates are coming back. Everything was eaten. Your creations were well received.'

Munny snorted. He was genuinely pleased about that, and it mitigated his disappointment and anger about the mistake.

Late that evening, as he and Dang and the surly southern European were cleaning up the kitchen, washing bowls and stoves, and the work was almost done, Luc entered the kitchen with a stony expression. He had a stocky build, and his round face usually seemed quite likeable. Behind round glasses, Luc now glared at him.

He jerked off his apron and carelessly threw it into a corner. 'Munny, you come with me.' He led him into a storage room for vegetables of all kinds and closed the door behind them.

Munny bowed his head. He gazed at the floor with a disgruntled expression.

'God damn it to hell!' Luc drew in a noisy breath and slapped his hand loudly on a shelf.

Munny winced.

'This kind of damn nonsense must not happen. You have to keep your eyes open! What if someone on your team goes crazy and scatters drawing pins over your starters?'

Luc's neck got redder and redder, and the veins in it bulged visibly. Munny rarely saw Luc, and to be so close to him, especially in this state, frightened him.

'What happened today must never happen to you again, the head waiter is absolutely right about that.'

Munny swallowed, dry-mouthed. So much for his job at Raffles. He considered taking off his apron and leaving right then and there.

'Damn it!' Luc ran a hand through his hair in exasperation. 'Yes, in the rush, mistakes can happen, but in our business, we have to make sure to keep them to a minimum. Still, we will say goodbye to the apprentice when he finishes his training. That's in a month. It's clear to me that if you'd had someone else at your side, this wouldn't have happened. He's caused us all a lot of headaches and mishaps.'

Munny gritted his teeth and stared at the black and white tiles on the floor.

After a long pause, Luc suddenly grinned, his mood reviving

just as quickly as his anger had come. 'But you and Dang, you did a very good job. I think you two make a good team. I'll have to take that into account when assigning you in the future.'

Munny looked at Luc open-mouthed.

Luc scratched his chin. 'Your compositions were very harmonious and went down well with the guests. Well done.'

Munny looked Luc in the eye for the first time.

Luc smiled and nodded at him. 'I would like to adapt my creations more to the old Khmer tradition. Do you think you could go over next week's suggestions? A kind of Eurasian fusion cuisine.'

Munny stuttered, smiling in amazement, 'I'd love to.'

In the kitchen, they had always said that Luc's outbursts of rage came out of nowhere. Now he had been on the receiving end himself for the first time. He didn't want to experience it again.

'I'll give you my ideas tomorrow. They're secret, of course, and not meant to be shared. I'm counting on you. Just give me some feedback, and we'll sit down together. By the way, my sous-chef was also very impressed with you.' Luc turned around, whistling a tune. His anger had evidently evaporated. 'See you tomorrow.'

Munny stayed in the storeroom. Minutes later, he could still hear the blood rushing in his ears.

Dang peeked through the door after what seemed like an eternity. Then he was startled when the door was yanked open.

'Are you spending the night there, or are we going for a beer round the corner?' Dang sounded quite amused. 'My goodness, you look as serious as a submarine!'

'A beer? Good idea.' Munny exhaled with relief. 'I just have to tell you what happened with Luc.'

Dang shook his head cheerfully. 'Am I going to be fired or assigned to cleaning duty?'

Munny laughed. 'Even better.'

'Oh dear, then I'd better go home and have a good cry.' Dang grinned. He had an admirable calmness about him. Voramay would have liked him. He never accepted that a thing was impossible. He always had a solution to hand.

That evening, Munny fell into bed exhausted but happy – not least because he believed he had finally found himself a good friend again.

V. THE CHALLENGE

Over the next few days, Munny devoted himself to Luc's assignment.

After he had documented all his notes in detail, he sealed the envelope and took it, together with Voramay's old book, to Luc.

Luc looked at Munny's suggestions with great interest and nodded repeatedly. Munny explained that some spices and roots could be used as medicinal plants, but were also used in ordinary cooking because of their bitter substances. Luc raised his eyebrows with interest. 'You got all that from the old book? Interesting!'

Munny beamed. 'My old friend Voramay inspired me with an idea. How about if, instead of the flambéed orange peel, we prepare a sweet and sour jelly cube made from fresh coconut juice to go with the duck. That would be a sensation!'

Luc laughed. 'You've really been thinking about it. I'll put you and Dang on my team next week. You can show the others how to use the new spices and ingredients.'

Munny strode out to tell Dang the news, his chest swelling with pride. For the first time, Dang was speechless and had no comment. He just said, '*Ooo*,' which in Cambodia means something like 'Wow'.

He and Dang discussed how they could cover each other's backs in the new team.

Munny wrinkled his forehead meaningfully. 'Dang, be a sport and make sure everything gets put in its proper place, so we don't have another disaster like the other day. I'll pay more attention too. Otherwise Luc will tear my head off. Besides, there are some people around who wouldn't want us newcomers to succeed, and could literally spit in our soup. Worse than having my specially prepared ingredients suddenly disappear or getting an order mixed up. You know what I mean.' Munny frowned and looked pointedly at Dang.

'Don't worry, after what happened last time, I'll keep an eye on everything, I swear!' He clenched his hand into a fist.

Munny nodded gratefully. 'Come on, let's go over the menu again and I'll show you what's important to me – or rather, what the special effect is.'

'Great, then I'll finally learn something – and hopefully next time I won't be assigned to peeling potatoes or cleaning duty.' He grimaced.

When Munny was standing in the kitchen with Luc's kitchen team, he showed them how to place the spices and the individual ingredients in separate small bowls. He explained the effects and the quantities, especially the order in which to do things. To his surprise, the chefs around him were very interested. He hung up information, small pre-prepared notes on a rail above the bowls, to make sure there was no confusion.

Dang sorted the ingredients for later, depending on the phase of the proceedings. Each starter could also be ordered as a purely vegetarian option at the guest's request.

So far, everything had gone according to plan. Now, as the team busied itself with the preparations, it grew quieter around them. It was relatively wordless but hectic work. Sometimes one of them would call out to the other what should be processed next, or signal that something was needed. After three quarters of an hour the taster portions were ready, waiting for Luc's approval, as they would later be served to the guests.

A little later, Luc cut the duck breast into fine slices and arranged them on the plate with flowers on a bed of wild asparagus, together with the jelly cubes made from fresh green coconut juice. That was the main course. The chefs on his team and Finn stood around the sideboard with their arms folded, waiting for his verdict. Finn winked at Munny, pleased. Munny and Dang were extremely curious to see how their herb-based appetisers would be received, and how Luc would rate the newly styled sauces with the new Khmer ingredients.

Luc nodded approvingly at almost every course. He only turned to Munny when it came to a sauce intended for an intermediate course which Munny had not made. 'There's a little too much bitterness in this. Is there anything we can do to counteract it?'

Munny nodded and grinned. 'Certainly, how about the home-made guava syrup? It's not too sweet. Or my homemade, slightly sweet coconut jelly. What do you think?'

'Okay, try both and use the one that tastes more rounded. Please document this for next time.'

A little later, they had the starting signal from the restaurant. Everyone started to work at once like clockwork. Finished dishes were brought to their places for pickup. Woks and pans were swivelled and prepared for the next use. Munny enjoyed this hustle and bustle, surrounded by exotic scents, tremendously. He smelled the fascinating ingredients. This was exactly what he had always wanted and dreamed of.

His eyes met Dang's, and they grinned contentedly at each other. Everyone was dripping with sweat. It was a real backbreaking job in the heat and the humid, hot vapours, with everyone crowded together in the confined space.

This day, Munny was very curious about the guests' reactions. Luc was putting the finishing touches on a few of the courses, while glancing around to check on everything that was going on in the kitchen.

Everything seemed to be to his satisfaction. Munny and Dang watched intently out of the corner of their eyes. They also saw how he made small, silent adjustments to straighten out the sequence of operations now and then. Munny admired this and made mental notes as well as he could. Finn grinned when he saw the two friends taking an ambitious interest.

When the pastry chef handed over his creations to the head waiter in the last phase, the rest of the kitchen team was just cleaning up the workstations and equipment.

Finn called out two Chinese names and assigned the people in question to the final clean-up. Munny and Dang looked at each other in amazement. Dang clicked his tongue and gave him a wink as he pushed an elbow into his ribs. 'We're out of here!'

Munny gave him a nudge. 'I thought you were volunteering.'

Dang chuckled. 'I'd need a few outstandingly pretty girls as an incentive.'

The head waiter returned with the first empty main course plates and announced with a complacent smile, almost as if he had been responsible for the dishes, that the guests would like to see the chef de cuisine before dessert. Luc smoothed out his jacket and checked to see if it was spotless, as indeed it usually was.

When he went out into the restaurant, the team in the kitchen heard the guests applauding unanimously. The kitchen staff all laughed and slapped each other on the back, the stress visibly dropping away from all who had been involved. Munny peered through a window into the dining room where Luc was bowing his thanks, visibly moved.

When Luc returned, he looked at Finn. 'Tell me, do we still have two bottles of that French champagne, or have you already drunk it all yourself?'

The team laughed.

Finn winked at Luc. 'I knew you'd need those last two bottles just for today. I saved them for you.' He disappeared into the cool room and came back grinning, holding the bottles. 'I knew it! Boa Bang, do we have any clean champagne glasses lying around somewhere? We're thirsty.'

A moment later, a number of filled glasses were standing on the cleaned kitchen island. Luc went to the front and grabbed one of them. 'Help yourselves. I would like to give my team a big compliment tonight. You worked together in a focused manner today, didn't make any mistakes, and no one was accidentally stabbed in the heat of the moment.'

Everyone laughed.

'Our guests from the gala party gave us special praise for our creations, as did the hotel management, who were also present today, and I am happy to pass it on to you.'

A slight murmur went through the team. 'I would like to give a special thanks to Munny. He hasn't been with us for long. But he showed me a few new things from traditional Khmer cuisine that added the final touch for a good many dishes.'

Everyone looked at the embarrassed Munny, who was standing there with his ears red.

Luc raised his glass. 'To our team! To you! Thank you very much!'

Dang looked at Munny and gave him a kick in the leg. 'Hey, if you keep standing there looking so sheepish with your red ears, I'll have to get a big bag and put it over you. Not a pretty sight! But cheers, anyway! My first champagne.'

Munny raised his glass to Dang. 'My first too.' He almost choked as he took a large foaming gulp.

When Finn and Luc came by the kitchen on their rounds, they clinked glasses with the two of them. Luc nodded approvingly.

'You did very well, you two. Munny, that was a splendid flawless performance. You work very well together.'

'Yes,' Finn said, eagerly nodding. 'Munny, the flavour genius, and Dang, the organisational talent – just keep it up! I think we should enter you in the next Raffles Group cooking competition, which is going to be televised. What do you think, Luc?'

'Why yes,' said Luc, his eyes widening. 'That could be something. You could definitely get on the shortlist for Raffles young chefs.'

Dang grinned at Munny. 'If he doesn't rip my head off when I forget his marinade.'

Munny elbowed Dang in the side, embarrassed.

Luc and Finn grinned. 'Cheers, you two!'

Almost all the chefs and kitchen helpers came over to Munny and raised their glasses to him, laughing. Munny, who had never drunk champagne before, was almost drunk as a result of that one glass.

'Hey, you can't hold your liquor, any more than a five-year-old. You need some practice.'

Dang quickly refilled his glass.

'Dang, go slow. This stuff really goes to my head.'

Dang laughed. 'Better than having Luc's praises going to your head! Come on, there's still some bread over there.' Dang tilted his head in the direction of a bread basket. 'We've none of us eaten much today, let's take some with us. It's better than nothing.' He walked away, but turned around abruptly. 'Hey, shall we go to the night market around the corner for dinner later? How about a really good *amok* to celebrate?'

'I'd love to, I'm starving. I haven't eaten since eight o'clock this morning.' He looked down with amusement at Dang, who was a head and a half shorter than him.

'Okay, I'll order you a rickshaw.' They laughed with relief and

74

carried on chatting with the others for quite a while. It was actually the first time that their colleagues had related to them in a personal way.

With all its little stalls for everyday needs, the night market was a lively place. They were able for the first time to talk at length, in one of the many small food stalls, about their origins, their families and how their fate had brought them to Raffles. There had never really been time before. The hectic pressure of the hotel kitchen kept them too busy.

The traditional chicken *amok* was filling and satisfied their empty stomachs. With a full belly and another beer on the way, they felt completely relaxed and serene, and laughed a lot.

'I say, Munny, I'm really enjoying having a buddy in the hotel. Somehow everyone there is a bit of a lone wolf.' Dang nodded contentedly and beamed at Munny.

'Dang, I feel the same way. I'm glad I found someone to talk to. Starting at Raffles was a bit of a cold shower for me.' Munny told his friend that he was a foundling, picked up off the streets as a baby with no knowledge of his real parents. He told him about the shock of his best friend Boran's death and how much this had affected him, and finally how he came to cooking through Voramay and how Paul had brought him to Raffles.

Dang nodded sympathetically. 'It wasn't easy for you either. Be glad you have such a great family behind you.' Dang lowered his gaze and his face looked grim. 'I come from a village near Nha Trang on the east coast of Vietnam. My father drank and beat me black and blue every time he came home. He was a fisherman. He beat my mother, too. Like me, she was afraid of him.'

Munny's eyes widened in shock.

Dang nodded meaningfully. 'Well, the problem was that she couldn't earn enough to support us both so we could get away from him. When I was fifteen, she gave me a little money and said that she wouldn't be coming back from the market that day. She told me to muddle my way through to Phnom Penh in Cambodia by land. She said that relatives of ours lived in the city. In my naivety, I thought it would be a village as idyllic as my own. I must have looked pretty stupid, crawling out of a lorry as a stowaway, with thousands of people swarming around me. So I wandered about the streets looking for work and food.'

Munny shook his head incredulously.

'Eventually the authorities picked me up on the street one evening and took me to a police station. I told them that I was Cambodian and had no parents. Well, it was almost true. They then took me to some nuns who had a school. They gave me food and a bed for the night. During the day, I had to help wherever they needed me at school. I also learned a bit there. I had managed to learn reading and writing at school before my father went completely off the rails. That was a great advantage. Many of my fellow students at the nuns' school were completely illiterate. Eventually I was allowed to do the shopping for the school kitchen because I could do arithmetic.'

Munny looked at him questioningly. 'Didn't you feel incredibly lonely?'

Dang just shrugged. 'What else could I do? When I was sixteen, I wanted to study. But they had to apply for a passport for me first. I was, after all, undocumented. After a nuns' meeting near Battambang, the mother superior of our school came back and asked me if I would like to go to Siem Reap. They were looking for someone to help in the kitchen. I joined the next nuns going there, and luckily ended up at Raffles – about two years before you joined us.'

Dang took a good swig from his beer bottle and scratched thoughtfully at the sodden label. 'I was damn lucky. A lot of things could have gone pretty wrong. Sometimes I was really close to the edge.'

Munny shook his head in shock. Thanks to Dang's story, he was more grateful than ever that his destiny had given him good and caring foster-parents. Of course, Dang had seen much more of the world than he had. But to be honest, he still wouldn't want to trade places with him. He admired the fact that Dang had remained such a positive character, full of zest for life, despite his difficult background. What a self-confident survivor he was, one who understood the art of living!

Both of them continued to reflect on their different fortunes for a few minutes. Then Dang suddenly pulled him out of his thoughts. 'But hey man, just think how well we did today! Who would have thought it? Did you expect that?'

Munny took a sip from his beer bottle and shook his head cautiously. 'No, I thought that progress in a place like this would be slow. And after the thing with the lamebrain apprentice, I felt like I'd blown it anyway. I actually have Chinese appetiser chef Bao Bang to thank. If he hadn't fallen sick, I would never have got away from the eternal vegetable chopping. And Finn probably put in a good word with Luc.' He took another sip. 'Yes, you're right. We were both lucky. Voramay would call that good karma.' He smiled, thinking of his old friend.

Dang smiled, lost in thought, and gave him a nod.

The next morning, they were assigned to the starters together with the starter chef Bao Bang. Finn had a group of foreign managing directors from international hotels, many of them from Europe and including some from the Raffles Group, as guests at the hotel for the next few days.

Finn had admonished everyone at his, as he called it, 'morning roll call' (also speaking on behalf of Luc at the kitchen meeting), that they were not to make any mistakes. The reputation of the hotel was at stake, along with that of the management. 'Today I have given the menu the title "Europe meets Cambodia" in honour of our guests. So no prizes for guessing that it's fusion cuisine. You have to give your all today and pull out all the stops! Does everyone understand that?!' With his glasses pushed up to the hairline, he furrowed his brow and looked seriously at the group.

Luc's menu that day was actually quite complicated. But you could already see that he drew his inspiration from Cambodian-style nouvelle cuisine.

Munny was very pleased that 'his' ingredients, which he had introduced with the help of his ingenious book, kept turning up. Inspired by Finn's earnest words, the whole team did their best. Luc and the management had to present the hotel kitchen to the guests, who were at the pool house at the time. He only came to the kitchen shortly before the starting signal in the evening, to check that everything there was in order. He then worked for a short time and did a few important tasks himself.

It was a hectic evening, as always. Munny was working on several creations that were new and exciting for him. To his delight, the new version of the foie gras he had formulated, with the jelly, was once again included in the menu.

They all had to work their utmost, and were visibly relieved when, after what felt like an endless working day and many beads of sweat on their foreheads, the desired applause finally rang out from the restaurant.

Luc, who had attended the dinner at the management table in the restaurant, bowed gratefully to the assembled company. He beamed proudly.

Munny and the other team members in the kitchen could see through the kitchen windows that he was also visibly relieved.

The next four days were the same. At lunchtime, Munny was assigned to prepare lunch outside in the hotel park with Finn and the various chefs. The guests were mostly small groups of hotel management staff who had declined to take part in the excursions offered. Perhaps they were too much involved in business discussions with their hotel colleagues.

On the last two days, a gala dinner was planned in the park by the beautiful big old pool to round off the event. It was going to be a real challenge for the kitchen, everyone was aware of that.

Munny was scheduled as the starter chef for these days. He was bursting with pride. The usually so relaxed Dang could hardly contain his excitement. The two of them went all out, and Munny once again consulted the special book Voramay had given him.

The result was exotic Khmer creations combined with European nouvelle cuisine. Dang was satisfied with the end result. 'I think this makes the grade, don't you?'

The two looked at each other with satisfaction. When they presented their creations to Finn and Luc, the two bosses were thrilled.

'We've never had it like this before, have we?' Luc looked at Finn questioningly. Finn nodded, almost in disbelief. 'This is amazing. You know what, we'll put all your creations on the plates, only in smaller portions. Let's see what the verdict is.'

The enthusiasm for Munny and Dang's work couldn't have been greater. After the first few courses, Finn came grinning into the kitchen. 'Munny, they're asking about you. Go out to the first round table on the right. There are two CIOs from our Raffles Group in Paris and London sitting on the left. One of the men at the table is the managing director of a well-known partner hotel in Sydney. He wants to meet you too.'

Munny's face glowed. 'I'd like to take Dang with me. I couldn't have done it without him.'

'If you must, you must – but don't let anyone poach you,' Finn warned him, grinning.

At the table Munny's cooking skills, in particular his knowledge of Khmer cuisine, were duly praised and belauded. In answer to their questions, he explained the basic principle of this cuisine, with its special ingredients and 1500-year-old tradition of healing knowledge. The hotel managers were interested and astonished. The enthusiasm of the dinner guests showed that the evening had been a complete success. Just as Munny was about to leave, Finn stopped him. 'Listen, I'm reluctant to tell you this.'

Munny was shocked, thinking Finn was about to criticise him.

'Each of those three from the table out there, the ones you talked to, has asked me whether you would be interested in working for them as a sous-chef for a year. That would be a real blow for us, of course, as you've already made a name for yourself and our cuisine.'

Finn pulled a long face and fiddled with a shirt button. 'But I want to be fair. When you're in your mid-twenties, you have to see something of the world. If you receive offers like this, even if they are to the detriment of your own hotel, you should still give it some thought.'

Munny looked at Finn, speechless. It was better not to say anything now and wait to see what came next. Finn looked at him over the rim of his glasses. 'But I would advise you to gain more experience first. As I said before, the best thing would be the annual cooking challenge organised by the Raffles Group. You should give that a go. I think it would really have something to offer you.'

Munny was quite surprised that his skills had attracted so much attention.

'The management has signalled its approval for me to select

you for next year. The challenge will take place in Singapore in nine months, and 34 other chefs, from our hotels around the world, will be taking part. It's a tough assignment. But if you're not afraid of competition or of the other competitors, I'll give the management the green light for you – and of course for Dang, who will be your assistant in the background.'

Munny had to smile at the thought.

'You would represent Cambodia in the competition. What do you say?' asked Finn.

Munny was speechless, his mouth hanging open in amazement.

Dang came out of the locker room around the corner. Grinning, he dug an elbow in his ribs. 'You still hungry? You look like a fish begging for food.'

Munny, still with his mouth open, shook his head in disbelief. Dang looked questioningly at Finn. 'Did he eat something that didn't agree with him?'

Finn laughed at the remark. By now, Dang could afford such insinuations without being reprimanded.

'I'll have to digest that first,' Munny said.

Dang grinned from ear to ear. 'So it was something you ate, was it? Come on, let's go and get ourselves something decent at the old market.'

He looked from Finn to Munny. 'What is actually up with him?'

'Come on,' Munny told him, 'I'll explain over a beer.'

Finn waved at the two of them as they left.

When Dang learned what it was about, he was just as speechless as Munny had been before. 'Man, I'll finally get out of this place and see other countries. I could really use a change of scene. Great!' He rubbed his hands enthusiastically.

Munny shook his head, uncertainly. 'Hey Dang, don't

underestimate this. It is a huge challenge and could quickly lead to defeat for both of us, undoing all our previous success.'

Dang, however, was full of enthusiasm and drive. 'Man, come on, we'll do it together. You can totally count on me.' He shook him. 'Come on, give yourself a kick, or should I do it for you?'

Munny looked into the determined face of his friend and couldn't help but laugh. 'All right, let's do it!'

Munny struggled to make up his mind for two days before telling Finn they would enter the competition. Voramay and his parents had a not insignificant influence on his decision.

Finn trained him several times a week before or after work, or on the few days off he had each month. He learned various techniques, from cutting to cooking and presenting dishes. He was particularly proud to show Finn his own knives, which he had received from Paul as a farewell gift.

Finn nodded, impressed. 'Take good care of this valuable gift. These are unique specimens. Very hard to come by. Paul was very generous.'

Munny groaned as he prepared for the competition. He had no idea what new skills would be needed.

After eight weeks, his head was spinning, and by now Dang's head was spinning too. Every few days, Finn gave them additional reading for homework and checked on it during their practical kitchen days. 'You can't just make your own creations for the competition. The jury gives you specifications, a recipe perhaps, whether it's a starter or a main course, to be developed according to certain criteria, based on a specific shopping list and on a theme chosen by the jury. They assess your skills in various categories. You are given time limits for each preparation. You need a wide variety of flavours and innovative ideas, and there is also real internal pressure.'

82

Munny's pulse quickened. He began to have slight doubts as to whether he had underestimated all of this.

'Participants are eliminated after each round. This goes on for seven days. It's really hard and demands everything you've got. You need to be really fit. But I see you as a very disciplined and focused person. I think you can do it. I'll come with you and support you. Next week we'll rehearse under competition conditions, and I'll give you tasks to solve under a time constraint. Okay?'

Munny nodded obediently and looked at Dang, who for once had no comeback ready. Munny was very relieved that they would have Finn at their side in the competition.

On the day of their departure for Singapore, the entire kitchen team was lined up with Luc. Luc looked at him with visible pride on his serious face. 'Here is your first black robe.' The managing director ceremoniously presented him with a neatly folded black three-piece suit with gold embroidery on the cap and jacket, bearing the hotel's hand-embroidered chef's logo. It was beautifully made.

Munny suppressed his emotion. He had a lump in his throat and shook the managing director's hand without a word.

Dang too was given a black three-piece suit. He was the first to find his composure again. 'When we come back, I promise you, the black won't signal a funeral. Otherwise, I'll go back to scrubbing floors in the kitchen.'

Luc winked at him, amused. 'Just be careful that doesn't come back to haunt you.'

VI. SINGAPORE

When they arrived in Singapore, Finn familiarised him with the competition venue. 'You know, it's something of a psychological advantage when you already know your way around and have made a note of the procedures. Let's see if I can meet some of the jury members before the competition. I've worked with a few of them over the years. I'd like to introduce you to one or two. It's always good to know people.'

Munny was very impressed by this modern, bustling city. He had never seen buildings and façades like this before. It all looked extremely futuristic. He felt small and insignificant by comparison, like an ant.

The people here seemed to come from every nation. They were all very well turned out and fashionably dressed. Some were wearing colourful, richly patterned sarongs, others were chic and stylish. He was impressed by the busyness and speed of everything, which he saw not only on the streets but also in their hotel, which too was part of the Raffles Group.

In contrast to the many modern buildings in the city, the hotel seemed more like a relic from colonial days. He admired the old black-and-white photographs on the walls of celebrities and crowned heads from around the world who had stayed here as guests.

On the first evening, the three of them sat at the almost legendary hotel bar in Raffles sipping Singapore slings, which were first created there and have since been copied many times. Munny thoroughly enjoyed the exceptionally elegant and relaxed atmosphere. It was incredibly exciting to watch the people coming and going.

'Cheers, lads! Here's to a successful time in Singapore! Here's to Team Cambodia!' Finn raised his glass euphorically and looked the two of them in the face, putting his own face uncomfortably close. He pulled a piece of paper out of his jacket. 'Look, Munny, this is a compilation of everything that's important. And here on the next page, to help you remember, are a few things to go over again that you had some difficulties with during the trial period. Dang, here's your cheat sheet to help you memorise!'

Munny was beginning to feel excited. The two looked at each other. Dang laughed dryly and patted him on the back in a comradely way. 'If we don't bring it off, I'll eat a broom. Or even one of Finn's appetisers, right?'

Finn nodded gravely. 'Guys, you have to concentrate. This only functions with absolute teamwork.'

'Right you are, boss,' Dang nodded, more soberly.

Munny slept poorly the two nights before the competition. The excitement of the challenge and the high demands ahead of him weighed heavily on his mind.

Finn met the two of them for breakfast early that morning. 'Last night, after you'd gone up to your room, I met two of my colleagues from the jury at the bar. That's a good thing for you, Munny. I was able to spark their interest in you. It's a surprise for them too, every time, to see who takes on this challenge. So impress them with your abilities and your style. Go all out on the first day of the competition. You know, first impressions are always the most important.' He gave Munny a friendly pat on the shoulder.

Despite the excitement, Munny was, as he had been the day

before, deeply impressed by the venue. This was the Esplanade, Singapore's cultural centre. It was a bizarre yet very elegant building in the shape of a giant durian fruit, located right on Marina Bay. He couldn't help but laugh at the thought. It's a fruit that foreigners avoid because of the smell, but in Asia it is very popular in traditional desserts. What a twist of fate. This was where he would make his debut as a young chef.

The interior of the building was spacious and generously laid out. The competition was taking place in one of the large concert halls. Their team of three arrived very early. Just a short time later, the place was already teeming with people. Spectators, jury members with their ID cards around their necks, journalists and, of course, other competitors. Long tables with kitchens behind them had been set up for their use, with each participant having their own section. Pots and bowls, along with kitchen utensils, had been provided for each of the competitors. The jury itself sat at the head, opposite. To their left and right were rows of seats for the spectators, and at the very front were the press.

Large signs with elegant letters on the tables displayed the names of the participants and the label of the hotel they came from.

Munny and Dang changed their clothes and made a fighting fist. Finn led them down the long corridor past the tables to their place.

Finn was a great support and a calming influence in all the hustle and bustle. He explained the cooking and serving area with its various tools to them once again.

He nodded in the direction of the jury, most of whom had already arrived. 'There are eight jury members in total, seven of them chefs and one a well-known restaurant critic. I know most of them. They're all wonderful people who have a sense for new things.' He winked meaningfully at Munny. He gave a few brief details worth knowing about their restaurants and countries of origin, and Munny was very impressed.

A gong announced the start of the competition. Finn gave both young chefs a warm hug and pointed to the spectator area from where he would be able to follow all the action.

An envelope was placed at each workstation. In the first round that day, all participants were given the same task. Dang positioned himself at the back of the improvised kitchen and was responsible in the background for the technical organisation and the timing, so that Munny could concentrate completely on the preparation.

They were given a starter to prepare, Munny's speciality. Apart from the time limit, there were no further specifications. He was free to work as he pleased and was more than satisfied with the ingredients supplied. In no time at all, he had created an imaginative blend of Asian and European flavours, artfully arranged on the plate.

A little later that day he also mastered the second round creatively and professionally in the given time, using the ingredients provided.

With a face glowing with excitement, he awaited the results of the first day. His pulse quickened as the jury announced his name, qualifying him for the next round. Unable to contain his joy, he gave Dang a hug and laughed, 'Well, that was a good show by us both. I'm proud of you.'

On the fourth day, Munny noticed that the TV crews were more closely packed. Journalists from the local and now also from the international press were present.

Munny was interviewed for the first time by a local newspaper ahead of the quarter-finals. A television crew was following the interview in the background. He told them that he was proud and excited to be able to prove his skills in the quarter-finals the next day.

'Could we also get your assessment of the level of difficulty – and what do you think of the competition venue?'

Munny turned and looked into the incredibly charming smile of a young woman, probably a little younger than him, in her mid-twenties. She had a notebook in her hand and was taking notes on the details of the various interviews. She had a Eurasian appearance with beautiful brown-green eyes in a face with a light bronze complexion. Her hair was pinned up.

He was so overwhelmed by her astonishingly good looks that he stuttered and stammered at first as he answered her questions. He was afraid she would notice how much he was staring at her. Her smile had quite enchanted him. Until now, it had generally been the other way around. The girls had always admired his lively, sparkling eyes and his fair complexion, giggling behind his back and whispering and following him with their looks.

The girl introduced herself as Maryam-Jaya, a journalism student who worked for one of the major local newspapers. Munny tried to answer her questions with the most charming smile possible. He somehow had the feeling that he had known her for a long time. She told him that she and her newspaper had been following the competition since the second round, and would be back for the rounds leading up to the final. She smiled at him. 'Good luck for the next few days and see you soon.' Graceful and light-footed, she floated out of the hall with her team.

Munny's first interview stayed with him for a long time. Was he sure he hadn't said anything stupid? Had he stuttered and stammered too much?

That evening, Finn invited the two of them to the rooftop restaurant of a famous old hotel on Marina Bay. As they ate, they watched the impressive laser show on the opposite shore.

Munny shivered a little despite the warm temperatures. It could have been due to the physical exertion of the past few days of competition. Or was it the thought of the beautiful Malaysian girl driving him crazy? Was he in love? He felt confused, and only sporadically followed the conversation between Finn and Dang.

'Are you okay?' asked Finn.

'Sure,' Munny said, without looking him in the eye.

'We'll go to bed early tonight. Tomorrow we'll start the semi-final well rested!' Finn furrowed his brow and struck a combative attitude with his fist clenched.

The next morning, Munny felt like he'd been run over by a train. He touched his forehead uncertainly, wondering if he had a fever. He decided not to tell Finn and Dang about it for the time being. He needed to focus fully on the tasks at hand today. He had to pull out all the stops for the team.

When he was back at his old place in the hall with Dang, waiting for the start, Dang nudged him with his elbow. 'What's up with you, anyway? You're tight-lipped and pale around the gills. Is the excitement finally getting to you? Hey, I'm right behind you here and Finn's there too. So no need to worry, dude.'

'It's nothing,' said Munny. 'Probably just the excitement.' He shivered, although his forehead was getting hotter and hotter.

The gong struck a metallic note and the envelope with their assignment landed on their table. Munny forgot everything around him. Even while reading, he was already reaching for pots and plates.

The task was to create a starter and a main course. The starter was to consist of a small piece of pan-fried Wagyu beef with pak choi vegetables and soya bean sprouts. So the key to success here was the homemade gravy and the vegetable marinade.

He knew he had to conjure up an explosion of flavours. The main course was to be a fish with beluga lentils and another side dish of the chef's choice. Munny planned to prepare the dish with guava juice to sweeten it, plus a ginger-like tuber to make it slightly spicy.

He called out instructions to Dang for preparing the two courses. He worked feverishly and as if in a trance on the different flavour variations. He knew that it now depended on his knowledge of herbs and spices in combination with the ingredients specified by the jury.

His starter was picturesquely arranged on a modern white plate in front of him. Now for the rest of the main course. He still had five minutes. Dizziness and chills overcame him. He tried to get the better of it. He swayed and struggled to concentrate, forcing his eyes open.

Dang touched him gently on the arm and nodded encouragingly. 'Three minutes to go. You can do it. Don't forget the gravy with the kaffir limes. Pay attention!'

Munny's head moved almost imperceptibly. As if in a trance, he dripped the gravy onto the side of the fish fillet in the final step. Suddenly a few drops fell on the edge of the plate, leaving a long, ugly trail. This would lose marks for the appearance! Dang shot forward behind Munny, electrified, and managed to clean the plate just in time before the gong sounded. He groaned and rolled his eyes, then gave Munny a searching look. 'Man, what's wrong with you? You're completely out of it and you look terrible.'

'I'm so cold and I think I have a fever. I need to sit down somewhere.'

Dang's eyes widened. 'Just hold on for another ten minutes until the jury have been to your table. I can support you.'

Dang glanced at Finn in the spectator area, signalling that

something was wrong with Munny. Finn looked serious and nodded, indicating that he had understood.

Dizzy and barely able to keep his eyes open, Munny tried to control himself while the jury evaluated his two courses according to all possible criteria. Some of the jury members nodded approvingly and smiled at Munny. He tried to smile too, but his face was pale and waxy, and his smile seemed forced and visibly cost him an effort.

After the end of the assessment round and the jury's deliberation, Finn hurried over to him with a stool that he had managed to organise from somewhere. 'Dang, what's the matter with him?'

'It looks like a fever. I don't think the freezing temperatures in the hall agree with him,' said Dang.

Finn looked seriously at Munny. 'We'll take you to the hotel in a minute and get you out of here. But actually it is damn cold and drafty here in the hall. I must have a word with the jury.'

The time until the announcement of the results seemed like an eternity to Munny. He didn't care about anything in his condition – not even the results. His head felt like it was in a vice. He groaned softly to himself.

And indeed, the committee took much longer to reach a decision this time. After an agonisingly long wait, another gong sounded. Finally! The results! When the jury announced them, Munny didn't really take any notice. He sat slumped on his stool and closed his eyes. Everything around him seemed unreal, like a film. He observed his surroundings apathetically.

Finn shook him out of his stupor. 'Munny, you did it, you're in the final!'

Munny opened his eyes and mumbled something incomprehensible. Finn looked worriedly at Dang. 'Listen, you take him to the hotel and put him to bed. Then call a doctor. I'll talk to the judges. There's no way Munny can compete in the final tomorrow in this state. I'll appeal to their sense of humanity and under-standing and ask for a day's postponement. I'll see what I can do. I'll come later.'

Dang looked worried. 'Sure, will do. Damn. So close to the final.'

When Finn knocked on Munny's door a good hour later, Dang opened it with a long face.

'How is he?'

Dang shook his head. 'Well, the doctor confirms that he has a bacterial infection. Probably from the air conditioning in the freezing hall. The doctor gave him two injections.

Finn nodded thoughtfully, and looked at Munny, lying pale in bed.

'The doctor wants to come back later this afternoon to check on him.'

Finn cleared his throat cautiously. 'I was able to negotiate a day's respite for us. The jury has agreed to my request, and they'll raise the room temperature as well.' He shook his head cautiously. 'That doesn't give him much time to recover. But maybe the med-ication will be enough to keep him focused for two hours. Hmm, I'll talk to the doctor and see what can be done. I've also post-poned the scheduled interviews until the following days. Munny's illness has already got out to the press. The other finalist isn't too thrilled about the special arrangements being made for him. But in the end, he had to accept the jury's decision.' Finn scratched the back of his head thoughtfully as he looked at the dozing Munny. 'Call me when he wakes up. I don't think he realises yet that he's through to the final. Maybe that will cheer him up a bit.'

At around five o'clock the doctor was back at Munny's bedside, taking blood pressure and temperature. He was pleased to see that the medication was working and had significantly reduced the fever. Munny lay awake in bed, staring at the assembled team around him.

The doctor took his leave with a slight bow. Finn pulled up a chair to Munny's bedside. Dang had hungrily helped himself to a few salted nuts from the minibar.

Finn smiled at Munny. 'You're in the finals, Munny. That was an outstanding performance by you and Dang. The competition was really very strong. I was able to get you an extension until the day after tomorrow. We'll see if we can get you back on your feet for two hours.'

Munny stared at Finn in disbelief. 'Really? I thought I'd messed up big time. The last thing I remember was dripping the juice all over the edge of the plate. Oh man, that's never happened to me before. Damn,' Munny complained.

'Hey, I was just able to clean up your mess in the last three seconds,' chuckled Dang. 'They didn't notice anything. It's all good, buddy.'

Munny smiled gratefully at Dang and shook his hand. 'Finn, I'm so grateful to you too for what you've done for me and for this opportunity. I'll do my best not to let you both down the day after tomorrow, I promise.'

'That's what I call discipline,' said Finn. 'The doctor will give you vitamin injections again tomorrow morning and the morning after. He's confident that he can get you back on your feet.'

Two days later, on the big day of the finals, the venue was packed with spectators and the press.

Munny, still a little shaky on his feet but full of adrenaline, looked intently towards the press area. Is *she* here? He spotted her and her newspaper team in the stands reserved for the press. His heart rate increased. She smiled at him and gave him a shy

94

thumbs-up. Munny was elated by this small gesture on her part. Under no circumstances was he going to let her down.

The metallic gong sounded. Munny and Dang received the envelopes with the assignments. Munny frantically pulled out the paper, and they both studied the final tasks intently. His fellow competitor from Europe was no doubt doing the same.

The jury's instructions were to prepare an Italian-inspired main course with prescribed ingredients and three freely selectable side dishes, followed by a dessert of one's own creation. Munny looked meaningfully at Dang and tapped the dessert specification with his finger: 'of one's own creation'.

Dang grinned. He seemed to suspect that Munny was planning to create his special jelly from the tart juice of the green coconut.

'Semolina flummery!' Munny whispered to Dang, who knew from that what he could get ready in the moulds in the meantime.

The European contestant probably had a slight advantage when it came to the main course. Munny resolved to concentrate on Luc's tips for European cuisine. To make sure of scoring points with the dessert, he started it first so that it would be cooled down by the end and not run. Dang prepared the moulds for it.

Munny broke into a sweat while preparing the main course. He wasn't sure if the fever was coming back or if it was just the excitement. At Finn's insistence, the room temperature had been turned up so that it was a little more pleasant to work in.

Munny hurried to finish Armagnac sauce for the tagliolini with morels. He just had to fry the angus beef briefly and then cut it into three appetising cubes when it had cooled. While he was preparing this, he feverishly thought about his side dishes. Since it was supposed to be Mediterranean, he chose artichoke hearts with aubergine tartare and fresh, raw, artichoke cubes cut small in a special marinade made from meat gravy with a few drops of kaffir lime oil.

When he had finished his creation, it was garnished with fresh rosemary sprigs.

Thanks to the timely preparation of the dessert, he had his jelly cubes on the now cooled semolina flummery with cinnamon in just a few simple steps. All garnished with banana blossom and morning glory. Done. On this occasion he was perfectly on time and was able to pause to see how it looked.

He glanced over at his competitor. His main course looked much more creative than Munny's. However, he was struggling with the time and with his dessert, which obviously didn't want to keep in shape.

The long-awaited gong sounded, and Munny's tension fell away like a leaden weight. No matter what the decision would be, given the somewhat adverse circumstances he had given his very best in his own eyes.

With a few beads of sweat on his forehead, he looked over at Finn. Finn nodded in appreciation and gave him the thumbs-up. Maryam-Jaya looked over at him from the crowd and beamed at him.

The audience and press applauded the two finalists. Photos were taken. Munny and his competitor's creations looked breathtaking and were well coordinated in colour. Munny began to doubt whether he could measure up to his colleague in the main course.

The entire panel approached them and congratulated them, lavishing praise on both finalists for all they had done to get to this point. They asked Munny kindly if he was physically all right after the competition.

The first thing to be judged was appearance, and here the jury was clearly of the opinion that his colleague's main course was a cut above. They were neck and neck when it came to the starters.

But when it came to judging the desserts, the incredible suddenly happened.

His competitor's artfully layered panna cotta melted and ran as if by magic, almost as if it had a time bomb under it – and with it, everything that had been meticulously built up on top. Spellbound and speechless, everyone looked at the strange spectacle. Munny suspected that the dish was probably still too warm and hadn't had enough time to cool. After this accident, the dessert on its big plate looked like a modern expressionist painting. The members of the committee looked at each other, some puzzled, some frowning, and put their heads together.

A low murmur went through the audience as they saw large images of it on the TV screens. Munny felt sorry for his colleague. Nobody deserves such a mishap. The members returned after a long consultation and began the taste test. There were appreciative nods for both starters and main courses.

When they tasted the desserts, they were delighted with Munny's exotic jelly and its ingredients. The jury members tried to guess what these jelly cubes with the unique taste could possibly be made of. Munny enlightened them and earned astonished and appreciative nods.

A break was scheduled before the final decision, and furniture was pushed back and forth to make room for the award ceremony. The press stormed the interior and quickly took up position in an optimal place for a clear view of the finalists.

Cameras filmed the two young chefs talking to their teams. Interviews followed. In his heart of hearts, Munny had been very much looking forward to giving Maryam his first interview of the day. Again and again, he tried to make out where she was in the crowd. But he was repeatedly distracted because everyone wanted to know how he was doing after his illness. It had become common knowledge that he had been in bed with a fever. He received all the more recognition for his discipline in completing the competition.

Finn squeezed through the crowds to him and hugged him fiercely, almost like a son.

Caught in Finn's embrace, he finally spotted *her*! Maryam was standing with a cameraman, studying his creations on their plates. She seemed to be on very familiar terms with the good-looking cameraman. He felt jealousy well up in him. The man was explaining something to her, and she seemed to be very interested and, amazingly, knew quite a bit about it.

She kept showing the cameraman which camera position was best, and repeated Munny's explanations, smiling charmingly into the camera. Munny was quite annoyed by this intrusive camera which kept coming between them.

Are they together? His world fell apart. Damn!

Suddenly she turned to him with a smile and nodded appreciatively. 'I love these European creations more than anything.' Almost casually, studying the plates more closely, 'My father is English,' she added. 'So I came into contact with European cuisine at an early age. My Malaysian mother always cooks both at home, alternating the two.'

Now Munny understood where she got her charming European facial features from with their fine lines, which had fascinated him so much.

Dang and Finn were talking behind him and kept patting each other on the back in their enthusiasm.

A gong sounded, and a sonorous male voice on the loudspeaker announced the return of the jury for the award ceremony. The other contestant had returned to his seat, but he suddenly made his way over to Munny. He held out his hand. 'You were really good, a tall order for me to face. It's a shame what happened to my dessert. But I guess that's just the way it is. Shit happens.'

Munny smiled at him appreciatively and congratulated him likewise.

He waited tensely for the verdict, wanting the almost unbearable tension to be resolved.

Finn stood with folded arms next to Dang and Munny. Munny was breaking out in a sweat again, and he was tired as well. He just hoped to get through it all in one piece.

The jury stood up solemnly and announced the individual points for each category. Everyone added them up in their heads. It was a real neck-and-neck race. The final point in the category of imagination and visual design – the jury was unanimous in its decision – went to Munny!

The audience erupted in thunderous applause. Munny looked questioningly at the beaming and laughing Finn. Dang gave him a shaking, laughing and wagging his head in disbelief. They both took him in their arms and squeezed him so hard that he almost lost his breath.

'Munny, you've done the incredible! You're now the best young chef of all Raffles hotels! What a killer promotion for our Raffles in Siem Reap! Man, can you imagine what this means for you?' Finn was beside himself and practically shook him like a wet rag.

Munny wagged his head, incredulous.

'Man, all doors are open to you now. Truly amazing,' Dang marvelled, hugging him and patting him on the back so hard that he coughed. 'Will you take me in your luggage to the world's hotels to be your assistant?' he grinned at him.

Only now was Munny able to take it in. Many hands shook their hands. There were countless group photos with all the media. Camera teams asked them for a lineup together with the jury. Notepads for interviews were whipped out. Munny beamed with relief all over his face, despite feeling waves of heat coming over him at intervals.

He scanned the crowd for Maryam's face. He hoped he had made an impression on her. But where was she? He searched for her, almost panicking. He really wanted to give her his phone number and ask her how long she was staying in Singapore. He kept getting distracted by cameras. Finally, Finn excitedly held a phone to his ear.

It was Ethan, the senior managing director of Raffles in Siem Reap. He congratulated him effusively. 'Munny, when you all get back, there'll be a huge reception for you at the hotel, I can promise you that.'

Ethan passed the phone to Luc. 'Munny, you rascal, you can't imagine how proud I am of you! I've got to tell Paul. He'll pass out. Enjoy the rest of your time in Singapore.'

Finn snatched the phone out of his hand and gave Luc an excited account of events.

Suddenly, when Munny turned around, there she was – this time without a cameraman. Her cheeks were flushed. Was she excited? She took his hand and congratulated him. My goodness! I'm in love, is that possible?

Suddenly she embraced him and gave him a shy kiss on the cheek. 'Congratulations. I really wanted you to win.'

Munny didn't know what was happening to him.

'Hey, champ,' she asked him, 'would you have time to join me in the editorial office for an exclusive interview?'

Munny did not have to think twice about it, but beamed at her with the most charming smile he could muster.

She pressed her business card into his hand with a wink and said goodbye.

Munny just didn't want to let go of her hand.

She smiled. 'See you tomorrow morning, then.'

Suddenly another hand reached out to him. 'I, too, would like to offer my warmest congratulations.' Munny looked into the broad, very attractive grin of the cameraman. His mood plummeted. The man looked stunning with his lightly tanned skin, and he was tall, as if made for a fashion magazine.

'I'm Julian. I work with Maryam at the newspaper. I gather you're coming to our place tomorrow. Nice to meet you. I look forward to seeing you then.' He gave a broad grin, revealing dazzling white teeth.

Munny no longer felt like smiling. Quite the opposite. He was deeply disillusioned and his mood dropped to rock bottom, despite his victory.

He watched the two of them for a long time, still feeling disappointed.

Dang had followed everything that had happened and put his hands on his hips. 'Hey pal, what more can you ask for? Just think about it, you're sick. And all the same you walk off with the title and maybe even the woman. What about me?' Dang poked him playfully in the upper arm.

'No,' Munny muttered moodily to himself. 'She had her guy with her and she's just left with him.'

That evening he, Finn and Dang celebrated extensively on the roof-top terrace of their hotel. After two hours, Munny went to bed, rather weak and still suffering from the fever. He had only allowed himself a small beer because of his medication. He didn't really feel like celebrating anyway. The disappointment of seeing Maryam with another man gnawed at him.

He set his alarm for nine o'clock so that he would be at the newspaper on time. He was really looking forward to seeing Maryam again, but for the thought of that young man who was attached to her. He slept like a log despite everything.

He arrived at the newspaper punctually at ten. He had been able to recover to some extent and was now feeling stronger again.

Having announced himself at the reception of the modern

newspaper building, he was taken to the lift and then to the editorial office on the eighth floor.

Maryam greeted him at the reception desk and showed him to a meeting room. As always, she had her notebook in her hand. She beamed at him. 'How are you? Have you been able to get some rest?' She looked at him with her beautiful, cat-like, sparkling eyes and put on that delightful smile again which he found so enchanting.

They had a lively conversation, but Munny was rather reserved towards her overall. He told her his life story up to the challenge in Singapore, and she was very impressed.

After an hour and a half, she closed her notebook and smiled at him. 'Okay, Mr Young Chef, I'll see what I can do with your story and the fascinating man behind it.' She winked at him teasingly.

What now? Was that it? Why was she looking at him so intensely, if she was already spoken for?

He plucked up his courage. 'Maryam, I would really love to go out with you tonight, but I think Julian would have something against it.'

She looked at him in puzzlement. 'No, why would he have anything against it? He may be older than me, but when it comes to what I do in the evenings, I make the decisions.' She chuckled.

Then, to his amazement, she nodded brightly. 'I'd love to!'

Munny laughed in surprise. 'Where and when?'

She thought for a moment. 'Do you know Riverside Point opposite Clarke Quay? There are lots of restaurants along the Singapore River, and it's always lively there. They serve food from all over the world, sometimes on boats. You'd like that.'

Munny agreed excitedly, his cheeks slightly flushed. He didn't care where they went, even a fast food restaurant would do. The main thing was that he would see her again that evening. They agreed on a time. He said goodbye with a smile, but still feeling a little uncertain. 'See you at seven, then.'

She waved charmingly at him, and they continued to look at each other for a long time until the automatic doors of the elevator closed in front of him.

Leaving the building he felt he was walking on air, but at the same time he was unsure what Maryam's earlier statement had meant. Despite everything, he was overjoyed, and he was smiling to himself when the phone suddenly rang.

'Man, where are you?' Dang asked. "I'm in a great rooftop restaurant on the other side of Marina Bay, having a cool drink. Are you done at the paper?' Dang's mood barometer was still at the top of the scale.

Munny agreed to meet him and headed for the nearest MRT station – the rapid Singapore metro, which connects the entire city and even goes under the water to the other side of the bay. He was constantly fascinated by this well-organised metropolis with its futuristic building complexes. He was particularly impressed by the mix of buildings and the greenery on the outer façades. A well-thought-out system, that also contributed to the city's climate.

Dang was sitting in an Italian restaurant on top of the Marina Bay Hotel, overlooking an incredible pool and the open South China Sea with its gigantic cargo ships coming and going.

'So, how was she?'

Munny made a deprecating gesture as he sat down. 'Well, it was just like an interview. She didn't have a chance to find out more about me yesterday, what with all the rush.'

'Come on, you didn't just talk about yesterday's challenge, did you? What else does she do? By the way, I think she's super pretty. Do you think she'd be interested in you?'

Munny shrugged, a little disillusioned. 'Maybe I'll find out to-night at dinner.' He gave a broad grin.

Dang's eyes widened.

'So you've already arranged to meet up! I guess I can come along as a chaperone?'

'You dare, you idiot,' Munny retorted. 'Get Finn to show you the sights.'

Maryam was wearing an Asian-style summer dress that fluttered in the wind, with a small stand-up collar. Her long hair was down.

She smiled as she held out her hand. 'Hi, champ, how are you feeling after the first twenty-four hours?'

He laughed broadly. 'Actually, I haven't really taken it in.' He would have liked to take her in his arms and never let go.

They walked along the quay past the various restaurants. 'Munny, you choose the restaurant you're most interested in, okay? After all, you're the expert.'

On a pontoon on the water, Munny saw a restaurant with the sign 'Cambodian Cuisine'. 'Do you know Cambodian cuisine?'

She shook her head. 'Not really. I'd like to try it.'

He chose one of the small bamboo tables on the riverside. A warm, pleasant wind was blowing in from the sea. Maryam asked Munny to order something typically Cambodian for her. He got them several appetisers on various starter plates, before ordering the main course for them both.

On the one hand, he felt incredibly lucky about the way his life was going, especially his being in Maryam's company. On the other, he didn't know whether she was just playing him, and would go back to her boyfriend's place tonight. 'Maryam, excuse me for asking this so directly, but I've been agonising over this question. I'd like to know how close you are with Julian. I would feel like an idiot if I interfered with you two.'

Maryam gave him a wide-eyed look. 'Well, we do work very closely together. And we've been living together for a long time, too.' She smiled mysteriously.

Munny had to struggle not to let his disappointment show. Maryam studied him and suddenly laughed. 'Munny, don't worry, Julian knows I'm meeting you ... Actually he's my brother.'

Munny's eyes widened in surprise. Only now did he realise how much she resembled Julian – they had the same eyes, and the same broad, friendly smiles.

His emotions went on a rollercoaster ride. He felt hot and cold. His cheeks were glowing. He actually had a chance! He would have loved to tell Voramay that thanks to the competition he was now standing in front of his dream girl.

They chatted intimately and laughed a lot. She told him that she came from a long-established and wealthy family. 'My father is an English publisher. He runs his business in London and has also had a presence in Singapore for decades. I was born here. My mother's family was involved in the founding of Singapore.'

Munny was very impressed and felt quite insignificant by comparison.

'I hope to end up at one of the leading business newspapers. Preferably abroad. You know, I was introduced to this field by my father at a very early age. I find it extremely exciting. Not least because it's also my father's hobbyhorse. He explained the workings of the economy to me when I was a child – or tried to explain them, at least.' She smiled. 'Since then, economics has fascinated me. Just imagine, I've been offered an internship at one of Australia's leading business newspapers. It would be a big step up in making a name for myself as a columnist. Dad was over the moon when I got accepted for the position.'

Munny nodded appreciatively. He had the feeling that she was endowed with the same energy and discipline as he was. However, her motivation was different. While he wanted to get out of his very simple environment, she could even choose her place of work. She had the freedom to choose. A situation he had always dreamed of, but one that his family could never financially afford.

Well, two worlds, he thought to himself pensively. 'When will you start your internship?' he asked cautiously. He felt almost fearful of losing sight of her again after this short time of getting to know each other.

'Oh, I'll work at the local newspaper for another month to finish my term paper. After that, I'll take a short break. I think I'll pack my bags and fly to Sydney in about two months. Will you come with me?' She laughed charmingly and winked at him.

Munny laughed back. 'If there's room for me in your suitcase, by all means.' He took her hand and looked at her for a long time. 'Maryam, I like you very much. I don't know how you feel about me, but I would really like to see you again, even if we have to go back to working in different countries in a few days.' He looked questioningly into her beautiful eyes.

She nodded and shyly bowed her head. 'Yes, I feel the same way. It would be nice if it works out. Munny, I like you too. Actually I like you a lot.' She giggled shyly.

Munny's heart was pounding like crazy. He took her other hand, and they held on to each other. Munny leaned over the small table and pulled her to him, kissing her tentatively. They were so absorbed in their mutual attraction that they forgot everything around them and only had eyes for each other.

'Come on, let's walk along the quay,' he suggested. She nodded, her cheeks slightly flushed. He put his arm around her shoulders, and they walked silently in the crowd along the Singapore River.

He stopped and turned her to face him. 'I wish we had more time together.'

She looked up at him and nodded silently. He wrapped his arms around her and kissed her passionately.

She took his head in her hands. 'Munny, I'm happy I met you. You immediately caught my eye among all the competitors on the first day. I think I fell in love with you there and then.'

Munny kissed her. 'And I'm such an idiot that I didn't even notice.'

They laughed about the way they had first felt drawn to one another. Holding hands, they strolled over to the MRT station. Maryam told him that she lived in the upmarket Tanglin district, just outside the city near the Botanic Gardens, and had to commute into the city every day.

Munny took her in his arms and kissed her tenderly for what felt like an eternity. 'I don't want to let you go, ever.'

She nodded and looked deep into his eyes. 'Me too. Will I see you tomorrow?'

Munny's throat was tight. 'Yes, definitely! Where?'

She thought for a moment. 'I have a break at noon tomorrow, which is usually an hour, but I can ask if I can stay out later.'

'I can't wait!' Munny hugged her and kissed her goodbye, as the train came in.

On his lengthy walk back to the hotel, he felt as if he were floating on air, his heart pounding wildly at the mere thought of her. Except perhaps for his winning the junior chef title, he had never before felt so happy in all his life.

Two days later, he was on the plane to Siem Reap with Dang and Finn.

The time with Maryam had passed very quickly. The next day, they had met up for a two-hour walk in the park and made plans. It had been wonderful to have her by his side. He already missed her.

Finn, who was sitting at his elbow, looked at him. 'You're not very talkative this morning. Aren't you looking forward to our very special reception at the hotel?'

Dang, who was sitting in the aisle seat, leaned over to Munny, grinning. 'He's so smitten, he's not with us right now.' He laughed uproariously. 'Idiot,' Munny grumbled.

Finn grinned too. 'Well, then our visit to Singapore was a complete success in every respect.' He looked at Munny and nudged him. Munny smiled sheepishly and looked thoughtfully out of the window.

They were picked up at the airport by the hotel's own limousine. The driver was beaming from ear to ear. 'The conquering hero returns. Congratulations to all of you, it was a great achievement. The word has spread all through the town.'

When they arrived at the hotel, the kitchen team, the service staff and the hotel management were all waiting for them.

The senior managing director, Ethan, came towards them with giant strides, beaming with joy, and congratulated them one by one. 'Look at this' – he pulled out various menus for the different restaurants in the hotel, and showed them, to their astonishment, the Raffles trophy label printed in gold letters for the best young chef. 'On behalf of the hotel, I would like to thank everyone. To begin with, this is an extraordinary achievement, and what is more it's great advertising for us, as you can already see from the booking figures.'

Luc and Ethan were both beaming.

Ethan approached Munny. 'We've come up with something special for you. Here, take this envelope. The time in Singapore was quite stressful for you, with little time for sightseeing. We thought you might want to revisit the scene of the action.'

Dang smirked and rolled his eyes. 'Please, not another challenge!'

Ethan grinned. 'No, we've booked you a week's R&R at Raffles, including spending money for the duration. What do you think? You know by now that holidays are unheard of in our line of business, but you do really deserve it.'

Munny laughed and shook his head in disbelief, fighting back tears.

He spontaneously hugged Ethan, who patted him on the back, surprised but pleased. Everyone laughed at Munny's unrestrained display of affection. Wow, he was thinking, that gives me a chance of seeing Maryam again!

Dang and Finn were also honoured for their tireless efforts. Their pride was obvious.

Ethan approached Munny. 'Oh, by the way, Munny, as soon as you've unpacked, please come to my office. There's something else we need to discuss.'

When he stood in Ethan's office a little later, Ethan offered him a chair in front of his desk and put on a tense expression. 'Maybe you remember the group of Raffles people in the garden for whom you prepared lunch?'

Munny nodded curiously.

'The two of our group from Paris and London, as well as the managing director of our partner hotel in Sydney, approached me and asked if we could loan you to them for a year as a sous-chef in their kitchens, as it were.'

Munny widened his eyes and stared at Ethan. Ethan just nodded and smiled. 'You obviously made a lasting impression on them. We would give you the green light for next year if you want. We would leave the location to you. What do you say?'

Munny was inwardly jubilant. He saw Maryam in his mind's eye, beaming at him as he delivered the good news to her.

Munny exchanged a few words with Ethan, but his mind was elsewhere. 'I'm deeply grateful,' he said as he left the office.

He called Maryam right away during his lunch break. It felt so good to hear her voice. Maryam laughed happily when he explained the situation. 'Simply incredible. I'm so happy that we'll see each other again in Singapore. I'll just take an extra week off work at the end of my internship, then we'll have time for each other and can discuss everything. And the other thing is just amazing. It would be great if you could go to Sydney. Then we could be together there too.'

She was right. He didn't really need more time to think about it. His decision was already made. He was glowing at the thought of their future together in Australia.

He told Ethan his decision that same day. Ethan nodded in approval and appreciation. 'That was a quick decision. I thought you'd have a harder time making up your mind.' He nodded affirmatively and promised to get everything in motion. Munny scratched the back of his head with a shy air. 'Could I take my partner Dang with me as a starter chef during my visiting year?'

Ethan raised his eyebrows and rocked his head thoughtfully from side to side. 'Let's see how we can organise this. It could mean pressure in the kitchen for Luc and Finn. They'll have to replace two people at once. But I'll let you know soon.'

When he told Voramay about his success and about his relationship with Maryam, she smiled knowingly and took his hands. 'You see, the good energy you have given to your life so far is coming back to you. Always trust your gut feeling and the teachings I have given you.'

She tied a homemade ribbon around his wrist and murmured mantras for him. Munny's parents were so proud of him and were beside themselves when they were invited to afternoon tea at the hotel. Munny led them past the reception to the park-like garden and introduced them to Finn, Luc and Dang, before whom they bowed reverently, which was almost embarrassing for him.

The time with Maryam in Singapore flew by. They were inseparable. Just a few days later, she stayed overnight with him in the elegant Raffles Hotel. It was so wonderful to wake up in the morning with her in his arms and gaze at her face until she woke up. They spent incredibly tender nights full of erotic passion, then enjoyed breakfast together on their private balcony each morning. Munny thought of the words of his spiritual mentor: 'Always trust your gut feeling.' He was certain that Maryam was the love of his life.

Maryam laid her chin on his chest. 'Let's make plans for how we're going to manage things in Sydney.'

Excitedly, they discussed their plans. Maryam's newspaper was based in northern Sydney and her workplace was a short distance away on the waterfront. So they would be able to see each other almost every day.

Maryam suggested they meet her parents. She wanted to introduce Munny to them over a traditional tea at Raffles. Her mother adored this English tradition.

Munny wasn't quite sure whether he would meet her parents' expectations. Maryam's stories were full of invitations and events. Munny's job, and even his recent success, seemed almost laughable in comparison.

'Don't you think I'm too insignificant in their eyes? I don't know if that's a good idea. And to be honest, I don't feel entirely comfortable with it.'

She waved it off with a laugh. 'Dad has always approved of my decisions. Wait until he meets you. Just be yourself. Don't worry. They were young once, too, they'll understand.' She embraced him and gave him a tender kiss.

Despite her reassuring words, Munny had a queasy feeling in the stomach.

'Look, in the end it only depends on the two of us, no matter what my parents think of you. You've built a great foundation for your own business. They have to recognise that. Everyone has to start somewhere.'

That afternoon at tea time, they were a little early at the reserved table. When an elegant elderly couple were led to the table by a hotel employee in livery, Munny's heart sank.

Maryam gave her father a tumultuous welcome. He looked like an English banker, slim and tall, dressed in a light summer suit. Her mother, in a close-fitting ensemble, had the same beautiful hair as Maryam, which she wore pinned up.

'You must be Munny, who our daughter's been telling us so much about lately.' Maryam's father gave him a broad smile and squeezed his hand in a firm, warm grip. Maryam's mother smiled gently and greeted him with a friendly lotus gesture.

After the usual pleasantries had been exchanged, Munny was relieved to see the trays of sandwiches and sweet pastries arrive, along with a glass of champagne for each guest. This was a welcome change from the very stiff atmosphere that had prevailed so far.

Maryam's father Daniel looked at him with a significant smile. 'Tell me, when do you actually find out that you have a talent for cooking? I suppose your mother was a fantastic cook?'

Not the time to talk about the humble soup kitchen, thought Munny. That would not sound too impressive in this elegant company.

'No, my Buddhist teacher recognised it in me early on and encouraged it. Ultimately, a book of hers was responsible, as well as the fact that I was lucky enough to be trained by a Swiss chef.

After my training came to an end, he got me my first job at Raffles.' He was sweating with agitation as Maryam's parents listened attentively to his every word. He hoped he wouldn't say anything wrong or inappropriate. He didn't want to let Maryam down.

'Your parents must be very proud of you now you've achieved success,' said Maryam's mother with a smile. 'We've visited almost all the Raffles hotels in the world for various occasions and soirées. You've made a good choice there. Raffles always has a special atmosphere, doesn't it, Dan?' Her husband nodded agreement. 'So how difficult did you find the competition? Did it feel like something you were already familiar with, or were you thrown in at the deep end?'

'Well, there were a few surprises. You had to be able to visualise the right approach pretty quickly.'

'You must be a real creative talent,' Dan nodded in appreciation. 'You should stay in Singapore. Then we could duly admire and savour your haute cuisine here. Celebrities frequently come to Raffles, not least for the cuisine. I even once had the honour, along with my wife and the Raffles president, of forming the reception committee for Queen Elizabeth II.' Dan confidently adjusted his shirt collar under his jacket.

Munny, in his lounge chair, felt very small.

'Oh dear,' Maryam said, 'was that the time you and my nanny parked me with my pram behind a palm tree, just to get me out of the way?' She laughed. 'Munny, my parents told me I screamed my head off in the lobby as the Queen walked down the line of honour. What an embarrassment! Even the Queen must have heard me.'

The whole family laughed at the memory of the incident.

Munny felt that this was a completely different world from his.

When there was a pause in the conversation, Maryam's father turned to him. 'How and where did you grow up?'

Munny was unsure what he should or shouldn't reveal about himself. He was afraid his humble background would make him look irredeemably bad in the eyes of her parents. Insecure and almost shy, he kept glancing at Maryam and told his life story in a few brief strokes. Maryam's mother looked questioningly at her daughter, silently stirring her tea. Altogether she didn't say much and mostly just nodded politely, smiling.

'I see,' Daniel said awkwardly, 'so you were adopted by your parents, so to speak. Your parents were really lucky that you turned out so well.' He rubbed his sleeve in an embarrassed gesture. 'There's no knowing,' he added in an undertone.

Maryam, painfully uncomfortable, shot him a reproachful glance. Munny's gut feeling was confirmed once again.

When he got to the point where he had met Maryam, a pensive silence fell on the table. Her father nodded thoughtfully and said a few appreciative words about Munny's making a go of his life. But it was not difficult to see that the parents were not happy with their daughter's choice. They had probably imagined something different.

'Well, it's a pity I didn't have a father with a hotel, or it would have been a lot easier for me, of course.' Munny couldn't help but make the comment. He was too irritated by the arrogant attitude of these people.

'We all have to start somewhere, don't we, Dad?' Maryam winked at him.

Dan nodded dutifully, while Maryam's mother seemed more interested in the guests at the next table and their clothing. There was a brief, uncomfortable silence.

After an extended pause, they traded some harmless pleasantries. Munny and Maryam exchanged a quick glance, and she signalled with her eyes that it would be better not to discuss their plans for Sydney just then. Munny understood why. After all, it was at Maryam's request that her father had established contact with his publisher colleague in Sydney. He could still change his mind and send her to a friendly colleague in London.

They said goodbye to each other in a friendly but reserved manner. He and Maryam were left alone. Munny looked down, upset and almost defeated. 'I told you so. I don't meet their expectations. They probably imagined a hotelier's son or a banker, but not a nobody who just happened to have a unique success.'

Maryam hugged him and looked at him imploringly. 'Come on, it'll be fine. They just have to get used to the idea that I love you.'

Munny laughed sarcastically. 'I can't imagine they'll do that in a hurry. What are we going to do if it gets out that we're meeting again in Sydney?'

She shrugged her shoulders almost defiantly. 'They'll just have to accept it. After all, I'm an adult.' She pulled him to her and kissed him.

Despite the wonderful time he'd had with her, on the flight back to Siem Reap Munny sat lost in thought and with mixed feelings.

In the following months, he concentrated fully on his work in the kitchen. This work had become very demanding. He was promoted to chef tournant, or head of a whole department. Dang also had his hands full. He was promoted to chef de partie, or section head, and was now the main point of contact for the kitchen staff.

Three weeks before Munny left for his posting to Sydney, Ethan summoned him to the management office once again. 'I wanted to say goodbye to you now, as I have to go to the Raffles Hotel in London the day after tomorrow. I would like to thank you again on behalf of the entire management team for your work here with us. I know what a lot you've put into it. I've spoken to the chef de cuisine and the management in Sydney. They've just let me know that your sous-chef will be missing for a long time due to illness. Are you still up for it?'

'Of course.'

"Well, then, you just show those Aussies what haute cuisine really means!' He laughed drily and gave Munny a firm handshake.

Only now did Munny realise how little time there was before his departure for Australia. Maryam had been in Sydney for two months and kept telling him enthusiastically how fantastic the city was, with all its possibilities. They didn't talk much about her parents and had decided not to tell them about their reunion for the time being. It seemed that her parents hardly referred to him in talking to Maryam. This confirmed his suspicion that they'd dismissed the relationship as just a juvenile flirtation.

Munny and Dang's farewell from the team at Raffles was unexpectedly emotional. In the meantime, Finn had been able to find a replacement in the kitchen for Dang's organisational skills, and so felt finally able to let the two boys go. Munny would never have thought that the entire team would come to seem so much like family. The staff kept making jokes at the boys' expense. Dang gave as good as he got, and relished their mock-indignant reactions.

Luc and Finn slapped their backs hard, not without some pride. Luc had just asked Paul from the Haven restaurant to let them have one of his best graduating students.

Munny hadn't thought that saying goodbye would be so painful. It only came home to him when he had to say goodbye to his parents.

That was even harder for him. And it was likely to be for a long time.

As a kindness to Voramay, his mother and father had decided

to meet at the Wat Damnak monastery to say goodbye. She could hardly go anywhere now because of her arthritis. It was heartbreaking to see how patiently she put up with the pain, while making light of it with boyish nonchalance.

Saying goodbye to his parents and Voramay was very emotional all round. His mother cried. He took Voramay in his arms and whispered 'Thank you for everything' in her ear. She nodded ever so slightly, her eyes cast down, and gently took his head in both hands, pressing her forehead against his.

VII. SYDNEY

Coming down to land in Sydney, Munny and Dang were impressed by the size of the city. Though it seemed very modern and bustling, it wasn't really to be compared with Singapore. He could hardly imagine finding his Maryam again in the crowds of people between the gigantic skyscrapers.

She had already told him enthusiastically on the phone about all the things there were to see and the things they absolutely had to do. She had raved about all the beaches and the nightlife. He was a little jealous that she had already been able to explore so much in the past few months without him. He, on the other hand, would probably arrive and be thrown in the deep end. To his annoyance, no time had been planned for him to settle in.

The old sous-chef at the hotel would probably be leaving in a few months. That meant the time until he took over was relatively short. So not much time to enjoy working together, he thought ruefully. He just hoped that he and Dang would get good support on the ground and be fairly received by the new team. The sous-chef had agreed to give them a detailed introduction before he disappeared from the scene, so that the leap in at the deep end would not be too gruelling. Munny thought this was very kind on his part, and was more than grateful for it. The Australian spirit really did seem to be as sporting and fair as the Aussies were said to be.

They took the train for Sydney Harbour where their new workplace, an upmarket luxury hotel, awaited them. The sun shone over the sparkling Tasman Sea, enough to raise the most doleful spirits.

They entered the gigantic and imposing reception area of the modern complex, expectant and a bit intimidated. After registering, they sat and waited on one of the heavy armchairs in the lobby. After a few minutes, a lanky, red-haired man, about six foot tall and around forty years of age, stood grinning before them. He held out a hand. 'Hi, I'm Liam, the chef de cuisine. I'm happy to meet you at last. Your reputation precedes you. Jason, our business manager, who visited you in Siem Reap, has told me some amazing things.'

Munny was extremely relieved to get such an easy-going guy as a boss. His boyish dry manner was immediately likeable. He shook his hand. 'I'm Munny.'

'Ahhh, the youngest award-winning chef of all time. You must be quite something. I'm really looking forward to finding out.' Liam's face broke into a broad grin.

Dang planted himself in front of Liam. 'And I'm his organisational genius, Dang.'

'Yes, I've heard of you, too. That's excellent, because we're sometimes lacking in organisation here.' Liam put on a pained expression, while winking at the two of them. 'Actually Jason wanted to say hello to you, too, I hope he still makes it before his meeting.'

They talked to Liam about the trip and their jobs at Raffles. He had followed parts of the cooking competition in Singapore on TV with interest, and was really looking forward to meeting the two young chefs. Jason had already told him enthusiastically about their encounter at Raffles, and how he had made Munny's acquaintance at a meeting with business partners.

As they were laughing about the misadventures at the competition, Jason hurried over to them. 'Sorry, I was delayed, I had to get some repairs organised. Munny, it's great to have you with us, a very warm welcome.' He shook the hands of the two newcomers firmly. With his light grey suit, dark blonde hair and impressive height, he cut a good figure. A pair of blue-grey eyes smiled warmly at them. 'It's good to see you again here. I'm especially pleased that you've chosen us. I heard you had a few offers from Europe to choose from. Liam will show you where you live, so you can unpack first. He'll also give you the other organisational details. Liam, can you please take care of them? I have to go to a meeting now. We will definitely cross paths again soon.' He waved as he left.

Dang and Munny had time until late afternoon to familiarise themselves with their new surroundings. They shared a small, bright apartment in the staff wing, and they were very happy with it. Munny would have liked to have Maryam in his arms right away, but the time until their first assignment in the kitchen would have been too short in view of the distance. He looked forward to feeling her close to his body the next morning, after the long time when they had only been talking on the phone.

Liam, who seemed to be a straightforward kind of person, immediately introduced them to everyone they met on their tour of the various areas of the hotel. It was an international group, with many young people who were mostly easy-going and relaxed with one another.

When the kitchen team arrived in the late afternoon, Liam introduced them to all the chefs and kitchen assistants. He explained that the menu here was aimed at their intercontinental clientele. Munny was looking forward to this. Raffles, while also catering for international guests, had always had an Asian focus. Here he saw an opportunity to deepen and broaden his knowledge.

He agreed with the old sous-chef that he would work closely with him for the first two days. That way he would be able to look over his shoulder and familiarise himself with the kitchen operations. At the beginning of next week he would then take over as sous-chef himself.

Finally, on the morning of the following day, Maryam and Munny were once again longingly in each other's arms. They walked in a park by the sea and kept stopping to kiss passionately.

Maryam told him how easy-going life was in Sydney. She had noticed that people here were less concerned with status than in Singapore, so that a delightful informality prevailed. She especially liked the omnipresent athleticism and appetite for life. 'Come on, let's take the train here and go to my place. I've found a beautiful apartment in the countryside near my publishing house,' Maryam enthused with a smile.

Munny grinned broadly and winked at her, after glancing at his watch. 'Sure – we still have almost three hours before I have to go into action in the kitchen.'

She nudged Munny in the arm. 'Hey, be careful what you say and do!'

He kissed her, smiling. 'I always am.'

She threw her head back, giggling.

Munny liked Maryam's spacious apartment very much. It actually had more rooms than necessary. They could easily live here together, if it weren't that it was a good half-hour away from his hotel.

Maryam pulled him towards her by his T-shirt and pressed her body closely against his. She enjoyed running her hands over the muscular torso under his shirt. He very much enjoyed feeling that she wanted him so much.

Happy and exhausted, Maryam lay in his arms. They considered how they could live together. They had discovered once again how much they loved each other and how much they needed to be together. Maryam wanted to find a suitable train or bus connection for him to the hotel, so that their shared desire to be finally living together could be fulfilled.

Munny quickly found his feet, not least thanks to the willing help of Liam and the outgoing sous-chef. He laughed a lot with his colleagues on the team. Even small mistakes were met with good humour – as long, that is, as they remained in the kitchen and were not passed on to the guests! He couldn't but remember his first blunder at Raffles, grinning inwardly. That had been a lesson for life.

On his days off, Maryam showed him the sights of the city. He was fascinated by the various modern architectural styles of the buildings, and by the different districts and faces of Sydney. In the small, quiet lanes of the old quarter, known as The Rocks, they usually stopped at one of the heritage pubs for a typical Australian snack with a local wine, or sat in the small, quiet courtyard of one of the many cafés and then strolled through the chic galleries and boutiques back to their apartment.

During their time together, Munny felt more and more how much he desired this beautiful and empathetic woman. He wanted to spend the rest of his life with her. However, he did not dare talk to Maryam about the future. The meeting with her parents still made him uncomfortable. He knew that they would never agree to her having a future with him. Their ideas of their daughter's future were too elitist. By speaking, Munny would only put Maryam in a difficult situation and force her hand. He therefore chose to delay this delicate subject a little longer, leaving it up to her when and how she wanted to talk to her parents about it. After all, the parents didn't even know that the two of them were now living and working in Sydney.

Dang often joined him and Maryam for lunch or a picnic on the beaches around the city. She had become friends with him immediately. She loved this carefree joker with his laid-back cheeky remarks. They laughed their heads off over Dang's first attempts at learning to surf.

Still, he quickly got the hang of it, his small but strong build helping him to maintain his balance. After a few weeks of ambitious practice, he was now able to cut a fine figure on the board. To Liam's amusement, Dang explained that surfing was part of the Aussie lifestyle and that now he was here, he absolutely had to favour this form of exercise.

Liam, the chef de cuisine, turned out to be a surfing freak. When he heard that Dang was learning to surf, he nudged Munny. 'And what about you?'

Munny shrugged his shoulders in embarrassment. 'I haven't got round to it yet.'

Liam looked astonished. 'Man, come to Bondi Beach tomorrow at eleven. You can rent boards there. I'll show you, Munny. You're a sporty, agile guy. You'll have it nailed in a few days, so you can ride small waves. I'll see you at the beach tomorrow. They've got beer and snacks there, too.' He gave him a friendly pat on the back.

Munny felt nervous when he sat on the board for the first time. He would rather have enjoyed some one-on-one time with Maryam. He was inwardly somewhat torn. Maryam however was thrilled by his attempt at surfing and was keen to join the three of them for a picnic, especially since she only knew Liam by reputation.

They enjoyed a great time together on the beach, and laughed a lot. Munny really got into surfing, and Liam seemed to enjoy showing them many useful tricks. Liam turned out to be a cheerful uncomplicated type. He didn't let either of them feel in any way that he was their superior. It was very funny the way Maryam and Liam teased each other and got into mock fights.

She was much amused by his tall lanky figure, which she found unusual for a chef. 'You don't look to be a good eater. Is that because of the quality of your cooking? Munny could give you some tips.' Liam pulled a face of pained reproach, and she threw her head back laughing.

He gave her a twinkling look and said, 'You watch what you say, or I'll make you a dish washer so you know how hard our business is.'

She giggled. 'And if I break a lot of dishes because I'm totally unsuited?'

'I'll just put you on a detox from Munny. He can work some extra shifts.' Liam laughed and slapped his thighs at the look on Munny's face.

Maryam looked at him, seemingly offended.

'You know what, Maryam, I like you both,' Liam explained, adopting a more serious tone. 'You belong together, I can tell. To be honest, I'm a bit jealous of you two. I haven't found the right woman yet. I guess it's a question of wait and see.'

Maryam patted his arm reassuringly. 'Liam, you're a great guy. Don't worry, you'll find your other half. Patience.'

Liam grimaced. 'You know, in our job it's difficult to find a partner who is tolerant and understanding. The working hours make it so complicated. When others are going out, we're work-ing. Stress is inevitable, like in my last relationship.'

Maryam nodded sympathetically and smiled at him. 'I could introduce you to a colleague of mine at the newspaper. She's really cool and very empathetic.'

Liam looked thoughtfully out to sea and mused in silence.

The months passed. Munny did an excellent job of familiarising himself with the hotel and its operations, using the knowledge he had gained and with the help of Liam's trust. Liam gave him a free hand. Meanwhile the hotel made a name for itself beyond the borders of Sydney with its experimental cuisine. Groups frequently booked the entire restaurant for an evening.

Reservations were now being taken several weeks in advance. Liam, Dang and Munny became close friends, not least thanks to Maryam, who introduced a fourth person to the group. Her colleague and friend Nicole was a kind-hearted person and got on extremely well with Liam. She was a caring, uncomplicated, well turned out young woman. Her roots were in England, but she had grown up in Australia and understood the not always obvious Australian mentality with its special brand of humour. Munny and Maryam suspected that the two had got together a few days ago and were already a couple.

One evening when Munny came home to Maryam after work, she looked unusually serious. It was her father's birthday that day, and she wanted to take the opportunity to tell him about her secret life with Munny in Sydney.

Both Munny and Maryam sensed that this would not be met with enthusiasm. Unsure, Maryam picked up the phone.

'If you think you can throw away your chances after all we've done for you, then go ahead. But you can forget about our support in the future. I wouldn't have had anything against a harmless flirtation, but when it comes to your plans for a life with your cook, you seem to have completely taken leave of your senses This is far below our standards,' her father snapped at her. 'It's all very disappointing for us,' he added testily.

He had never used such harsh and hostile words to her before.

Maryam looked at Munny, dismayed and speechless, as she held the phone.

'Your parents' door is always open to you when you come to your senses and realise what a bad decision you've made.'

She cried silently into the phone and begged her father once more, in a voice choked with tears, to accept her love for Munny. But there was only a click at the other end of the line.

Maryam wept uncontrollably. Munny had expected this, but he was as stunned as she was by her father's lack of respect. He took her gently in his arms. 'Sweetheart, I'm so sorry. I wish I could offer you a more well-to-do family,' he murmured in her ear. 'Maryam, darling, I don't want to come between you and your parents. I feel so guilty and responsible for this whole mess. If you want to go back to them or make a different decision, it would hurt me very much but I would accept it.'

Maryam looked at him with outraged exasperation. 'What? You would give in to them after they've been so rude? No, I can't do that. I'm not their puppet. If they think they have to break off contact with me because of this, then let them! This is my life!'

She buried her face defiantly on his shoulder. 'Munny, you're serious about me, aren't you?' she murmured against his arm, her voice quivering.

Munny kissed her tenderly. 'Dearest, you are quite simply the love of my life. I never want to be separated from you again.' He shook his head in disbelief at the coldness her parents were capable of.

He put his arms around her waist and looked deep into her eyes. 'Darling, do you want to be with me forever?' He swallowed dryly. 'Will you marry me? I'm making a good living now – we can easily afford a life of our own here, and you can fulfil your dream of becoming a newspaper columnist.'

Maryam looked up at him with a smile. After what felt like an eternity, she whispered a soft but definite 'Yes' tenderly into his ear. Munny was beyond happy to have found his own new family.

As Maryam snuggled up to him in bed, they discussed in whispers the arrangements for a registry office wedding. They were clear about one thing from the start: Dang should be Munny's best man, and Maryam, who originally had Liam in mind, decided on Munny's advice to invite her friend Nicole. She and Liam had been close for months, and the four of them spent as much time together as possible. Maybe everything would be all right after all, as Voramay was always telling him.

VIII. MARYAM

Munny wished Voramay could have been there so he could introduce her to Maryam. They decided to go to his parents' house in Siem Reap for a few days after their wedding. Maryam had happily agreed to his request that they hold a Buddhist wedding ceremony there with Voramay and his family.

When Finn in Siem Reap heard about the wedding, he spontaneously took leave to be in his hometown of Sydney so he could accept Munny's invitation. Munny was genuinely happy that Finn was doing him the honour of attending and that he would see him again. It was a good feeling to have an old friend at his wedding.

They had chosen a beautiful shady spot in the Royal Botanic Gardens for their wedding ceremony, directly under one of the huge old fig trees, also known in Cambodia as banyan trees, the tree of Buddha's enlightenment.

Munny had insisted on wearing a midnight blue suit with a tie – his first suit. Maryam wore a champagne-coloured, knee-length silk dress slit on one side, with delicate shoulder straps made of white pearls.

Her hair was pinned up, and with a white frangipani blossom in it, she looked breathtaking and very fragile.

Liam and Nicole approached them beaming, she in a light blue summer dress and Liam in a sandy-coloured suit. Munny turned around looking in all directions for Dang. He felt a little uneasy. He had reminded him the day before to be punctual. Liam nudged Munny in the side with a grin and nodded his head to the right. 'Will you look at that?'

Immediately everyone turned that way and saw Dang approaching them with a wry grin, the rotund marriage celebrant on his arm. 'I wanted to make sure that the most important registry office person wasn't missing. Wouldn't want the wedding to be cancelled so you'd have a reason to back out. It doesn't matter to me, but we'd all be sorry for Maryam.'

Liam thumped Dang on the back, laughing loudly. 'You're such a nutcase.' Dang gave Maryam an exuberant hug.

Liam turned to Munny. 'I hope you don't mind, but Jason and his wife came with us. They wanted to congratulate you too.'

Munny and Maryam turned in astonishment and saw a beaming couple approaching them. The hotel manager and his wife Alicia had insisted on being there. Munny was visibly moved by so much attention.

Jason gave Munny a bear hug. 'Congratulations!' he mumbled, with emotion. 'I wouldn't miss your most important day for the world. You can do what you like, but you won't get rid of us.'

The smiling registrar asked the couple and the witnesses to line up under the fig tree, and told Dang to have the rings ready. Dang fumbled with his jacket. Munny shot him a reproachful glance. Grinning, he managed to extract the rings from his inside pocket and shrugged, putting on an air of innocence.

The ceremony in the park under the morning trees was simple but very moving. As they slipped the delicate golden rings on each other's fingers and Munny kissed Maryam tenderly, he whispered in her ear, 'I love you so much and I want to be with you forever.'

Maryam, with tears of emotion and happiness in her eyes, could only nod and kiss him. They didn't even notice the thunderous applause that broke out. It was only when Munny turned away from Maryam and looked to the side that he saw that the whole kitchen team, together with the receptionists and the entire hotel management, had formed a circle around them. He shook his head, visibly moved.

He and Maryam shook countless hands. 'We wouldn't dream of leaving our favourite sous-chef alone on a day like this.'

Munny looked at Liam, perplexed. 'My goodness, who's running the place now?'

Jason laughed dryly, 'I took Dang's advice and had a sign made for the restaurant doors: "Closed for lunch".'

Another typical Dang move, Munny thought. Dang just winked at him, amused.

'We thought that you and we of the management could eat whatever you like to prepare – so today the five-star restaurant is ours for a change. Dang and Liam have combined forces to conjure up something for us all. What do you think?' Jason beamed proudly at him. 'This day is the hotel management's wedding gift to you.' He turned around and waved at the bartender and the hotel service staff, who were standing at the edge of the flowerbeds.

'Let's all toast the happy couple. We wish you all the luck in the world!' Jason raised his glass and everyone followed suit.

Munny and Maryam were overwhelmed. With a quivering voice, Munny just managed to say, 'Thank you all.'

Lunch, and the subsequent tea, with their friends all around them, was one of the best things about this day, showing how warmly and welcomingly they had been received in their new adopted country.

In a quiet moment after tea, Jason and Liam took Munny aside. 'Munny, we heard you two are looking for a new apartment.' Munny scratched the back of his head and nodded.

'Liam had the idea of letting you rent the hotel flat, which was used by the outgoing sous-chef and his wife, if you would like that. What do you think?'

Munny thought about it for a moment. Actually that would be the perfect solution for him and Maryam.

'The hotel could cover some of the costs,' explained Jason, 'since it benefits us if you don't have far to go to work. I think Maryam could handle a short train ride to her publishing house, right?'

Munny smiled, delighted that the hotel was being so considerate. 'Thank you for the generous offer. I'm pretty sure my wife would like that. I'll talk to Maryam about it.'

'Oh and, Munny, there's one more thing.' Jason scratched his head, slightly embarrassed. 'Your contract here is only for a year and expires in a few months. Think about whether you might be able to stay with us. I could talk to the management of Raffles in Siem Reap.'

'We could send one of our guys there for a year in exchange,' Liam suggested. Jason nodded in agreement.

'I know that Cambodia is your home, but couldn't you imagine running our restaurants together with me in the future?' Liam looked at him questioningly.

Munny was taken aback. They had got it all worked out. He looked at the two of them in turn, amazed.

'I don't think Maryam will have much trouble getting a good job in the city after she graduates,' Munny said.

Liam winked at Munny. 'And on your days off, surfing's the order of the day, mate!'

Munny couldn't help but laugh at the words. 'You bet!'

'Then you'll just have to break it to your wife gently,' Jason grinned.

Maryam didn't need much time to think about it. Just one day before her wedding, her boss had offered her a job as a columnist after she graduated in three months' time.

She would really have liked to tell her parents about it! But since the fracas, she had had no further contact with them.

She pulled Munny close to her. 'I thought you really wanted to rejoin your family in Siem Reap and go back to working there. But this is a wonderful turn of events. We've both got the best possible job prospects. Let's stay here in our new adopted home.' She kissed him passionately.

Four weeks later, they were able to move into the beautiful, bright three-room apartment that Jason had designated for them. It was generously proportioned, and they felt comfortable right away. Munny was proud of what he had already achieved at almost twenty-nine.

They travelled to Munny's parents for a week to hold the Buddhist wedding ceremony in Siem Reap as planned.

The ceremony began two days later in the morning at the Wat Damnak monastery. The two of them received the blessing of the head monk. Voramay had insisted on holding everything – the wedding, the ceremony and the party with all their friends – in the temple, and not in a marquee, which she thought was much too modern.

She congratulated Munny, beaming all over her face, on his Maryam, taking her to her heart immediately.

The time in Siem Reap passed quickly. Saying goodbye to his parents and friends was very emotional. Munny's family had taken Maryam in like one of their own, and had grown very fond of her. They were vastly proud of Munny's success and reputation and delighted that he had found such an elegant and beautiful woman.

Saying goodbye to Voramay, on the other hand, was a sad and tearful occasion. She blessed him again and tied lucky ribbons around his wrist. She smiled at him meaningfully, but her smile somehow also made him sad. 'Munny, my son, I can feel that the circle of my samsara will soon be complete. It is time for me to let go and trust my karma.'

He didn't really understand her words at first. What was she trying to tell him? He looked into her eyes. She nodded slightly, confirming his silent question, and squeezed both of his hands at the same time.

'Voramay,' he said, 'I'll be back soon, after all. I can afford it now.' He immediately felt like an idiot after making this remark.

She looked at him, smiling gently. 'Munny, this time I'll come and visit you.'

He understood. Impulsively, he took her hands and put them to his face, weeping without restraint.

'Just believe in our teaching and hold onto the things I've taught you, okay?' She closed her eyes, took his head in both hands in the calm, thoughtful way she had, and pressed her forehead against it.

As Munny and Maryam sat on the plane back to Sydney, he fought back tears. He knew this was a farewell for ever. Maryam took his hand, held it tightly and laid her head on his shoulder. He held her close, silently and gratefully.

Munny, supported by Liam, made a big name for himself with their Michelin-starred restaurant. Since Liam took over the management of events, Munny got a free hand in organising the kitchen team. A proud Dang, with a team of four chefs, managed the starters in all the hotel's restaurants.

Munny was very happy with his life in Sydney and with the great love of his life. Things couldn't have gone better for him, until five months after his return, he received the news from his parents that Voramay had passed away. Although she had gently prepared him for this, deep inside him he still felt a painful emptiness.

Liam patted his shoulder, when he saw the sadness in his face. 'What, trouble in paradise?'

Munny shook his head sadly and told Liam briefly about the death of his old friend and mentor. Liam nodded sympathetically. 'Yeah, you're bound to be upset by something like that. I know that all too well. Hey, I have an idea to cheer you up. Nicole managed to get four tickets for the Sydney Opera House tomorrow night. Let's all go and then have a few drinks afterwards. That would be really cool.'

'Very kind of you, good idea, Liam. I'll talk to Maryam.'

The opera was magnificent, and during the interval they stood together enjoying a glass of champagne. Liam told stories about mishaps at the hotel in the past. They all stood grinning together.

Liam was on top form. 'Just imagine the look on Jason's face ...'

'How dare you show your face in public!' A shrill voice interrupted Liam. Everyone in the room turned around in alarm.

'You murderer!' a woman screamed, her voice cracking.

Liam just opened his eyes in shock. The woman rudely pushed her way towards Liam through the people around them, jostling Nicole.

'What is the matter with you?' she exclaimed.

'Stay out of this, my girl,' the woman snapped.

'Well, Liam,' she continued, 'who are you going to kill next?'

'Rose, just let it go,' he said, trying to placate her.

Maryam and Munny watched the scene in silence. The woman was wearing a thin, matted pullover and a faded, long pleated skirt, from under which a pair of brown, worn-out shoes peeped out.

'Oh, you don't know, he didn't tell you? He's responsible for our mother's death!'

'Rose, get out of here! Why don't you just get out of my life for good!' he hissed at her.

'You'd like that, but I'll always be on your back, remember that.' The woman spat out her words full of hatred. 'You took my mother from me!'

Liam turned to his speechless friends. 'Let's go, I can't stand this anymore. My sister has been haunting and stalking me ever since the accident.' He pressed his lips together in exasperation.

Munny had never seen his boss so enraged. They left Rose, still cursing horribly, in the crowded foyer, and literally fled from the opera house and out into the open air. The woman followed them outside and continued to rant loudly after them from the top of the steps.

Maryam looked at Munny questioningly.

Nicole took an audible breath. 'Liam, whatever was all that about?' She looked at him with an earnest expression.

Liam sat down on the corner steps below the building. 'It feels like it's been an eternity, and that ... that...' he gasped, 'that beast of a sister still blames me for the failure of her life.' He was visibly struggling to find words.

'What's that got to do with your mother?' Munny asked.

Liam snorted and wrinkled his forehead. 'When I was seventeen, Mum taught me how to drive. I got the hang of it pretty quickly in her old Cherokee. My sister was fourteen. Dad had left our mother for another woman. So it was pretty handy that I could drive. That way I could take some of the load off Mum's shoulders with the shopping.' A tear ran down his cheek. He was visibly struggling with himself and shook his head again and again. 'We were out shopping, I was going to drive us back ... I started off as usual ... my God, I still don't know how it happened.

I just … I just didn't see it. Damn … Mum was still screaming, but … my God …' He swallowed hard with his head bowed.

'What?' Maryam asked gently, holding his shoulder.

Liam shook his head in despair. 'Then suddenly this other car was there and slammed into our side. They said later that I hadn't respected the right of way. Mum still looked okay. She just gave me a shocked look. But then she slumped down and fell forwards in the car. I didn't know what to do or what was going on. Rose in the back seat just screamed in panic. She was in shock. My God, it was so awful. At the hospital, they told me that they couldn't do anything more for my mum, that her neck was completely broken. She died in the car next to me. I'm responsible for her death.' Liam wiped away tears from his face. 'Rose never forgave me. Somehow her life never got back on track. She went completely off the rails and drifted around. She managed to finish an apprenticeship, with great difficulty. But after that she was never able to hold down a job for more than a year.' He sucked in a deep breath. 'She was thrown out of everywhere because of her aggression and rude behaviour. At first l supported her financially, but she always saw that as an admission of guilt on my part and took it as something she was entitled to. I stopped funding her after ten years when I realised it wasn't helping her become independent. But now she's stalking me and putting me in crazy situations!' He shook his head angrily. 'Hell and damnation! She blames me for everything!' Liam ran his fingers desperately through his hair.

'She should go into therapy and not yell at you like that in front of everyone and behave so badly. She should let bygones be bygones,' Nicole said angrily.

Maryam and Munny nodded in agreement. Munny pulled Liam back to his feet. 'Come on, let's go somewhere more comfortable.'

They left the scene of the incident. Nicole put her arm around

Liam and stroked his back tenderly. After a few drinks, they had got over the unpleasant episode to some extent.

On one of his evenings off, Maryam surprised Munny with a set table, beaming. 'Sir, may I invite you to a candlelight dinner?'

Munny shook his head in amazement. They usually went out with friends on their evenings off, or else to an exhibition.

She winked at him. 'Come on, sit down and enjoy my cooking for a change.'

Munny laughed. 'Oh dear, there's that saying: a cobbler should stick to his last, right?'

Maryam punched him on the arm. 'Hey, you're not the only one who can cook. Anyone can do it.'

Munny raised his eyebrows and grinned, for which he was promptly punched again on the upper arm.

'Is there something to celebrate?' he asked. 'Our wedding anniversary won't be for a while?'

Maryam smiled mysteriously and pressed herself passionately against him. 'I wasn't going to say anything until after dinner ... but I just can't keep it to myself anymore.'

'What? Have you been promoted?' She shook her head and laughed.

'No, Munny, I'm pregnant. Four months along.'

Munny shook his head in disbelief. 'Really and truly?'

She hugged him, nodding and laughing. 'Yes.'

'My goodness, I'm amazed. Unbelievable! Wow! We have to toast this!'

Maryam shook her head from side to side. 'Well, from now on only with water.' He took her in his arms and held her gently. 'I'm so incredibly happy, darling. You are the love of my life.'

IX. ESTELLE

'Munny, could you please pick Estelle up from kindergarten tomorrow at noon? I have to go to an editorial meeting at short notice tomorrow. I still have no idea how long it will take.'

Munny nodded. It was his day off, which he had negotiated after Estelle's second birthday. 'Shall we meet at Maroubra Beach at lunchtime for a barbecue? Estelle could go snorkelling there.' The little girl was already a real water baby at five years old.

'Yes, I'd like that, if my colleagues can wrap things up quickly. I'll give you a call on the way and let you know.' Maryam had taken a part-time job at her newspaper after Estelle was born.

Munny had come to a good arrangement with Liam over kitchen hours, and had enjoyed a certain amount of private space ever since. Their friendship had become even closer in the meantime. Liam and Nicole had married nine months earlier. It was obvious that Munny's and Maryam's efforts to get the couple together had been worthwhile. Munny had to grin when he thought of all the lengths they had gone to. Recalling this in his wedding speech, Liam had had a lot of fun at Munny's expense.

Munny's daughter Estelle was his world. She was the apple of his eye. Already a little beauty with her big dark brown, almond-shaped eyes and her shoulder-length brown hair, which shimmered like mahogany. He was incredibly proud and happy about how positively his life had developed, now he was aged thirty-five, all of it thanks to his Maryam.

She had found a good balance between her work at the newspaper and her little family.

Estelle, at five years old, was just as curious and eager to learn as he had been at the same age. He was fascinated by her and her precocious curiosity. Voramay must have felt the same way about him. He smiled as he thought of his former mentor.

Estelle was ahead of her peers in many ways. For example, she was already very good at reading and had colossal ambition in everything she did.

Maryam called him on his mobile phone when he arrived at his daughter's pre-school. 'Guess what? We've wrapped up the agenda, and they've come to a decision, believe it or not. I'm going down to the beach. I'll meet you there, okay?' she giggled, pleased with the early termination of what was usually an interminable meeting.

'Yes, I've just arrived at Estelle's pre-school. Great, that's perfect. See you soon, darling. I'm looking forward to it.'

When his daughter ran into his arms in front of the school, he tossed her up in the air. She squealed with delight. When Munny announced that they were going to the barbecue on the beach and that Mama was coming too, she threw her arms around his neck in euphoria. She was totally fascinated by the sea and couldn't get enough of swimming.

She thoroughly enjoyed her freedom on the beach. Despite the shade at the barbecue stand, it was oppressively hot, and she gradually calmed down and got drowsy. When they finally decided to go home, Maryam had to carry the little one, who was already asleep on her shoulder, to bed. Munny grinned at the prospect of some well-deserved peace and quiet. 'Now we'll finally have some time for ourselves.' He pulled her into bed, put his arms around her hips and kissed her. She laughed. 'I don't know what you mean.'

He let his hands glide tenderly over her naked body. Her skin felt like velvet. Between his hands and her skin there was a voltage, causing small hairs to stand up. She breathed in and out deeply with her eyes closed, stretching under his touch and wrapping her legs around his hips. He loved the way she showed him, in her own way, how much she desired him. Passionate shivers coursed through his body. Trembling, he gave in to her urging, and they made love intensely again and again. Feeling her body on his, the way she took possession of him, was extremely arousing.

Maryam snuggled into Munny's arms and pulled the duvet up. Her long, soft hair fell over her half-covered back. He ran his hand through her tousled hair. It always made his heart beat faster.

'Hey, shouldn't we put Estelle into school at the start of the next school year? She'll be five and a half. I've spoken to the teachers and they agree that she's very quick for her age and can hold her own with older children,' Maryam whispered.

Munny nodded and remembered how he had skipped a school year and had to leave his friend Boran behind in the old class. It had been hard at the beginning, but in retrospect it had been very beneficial for him. 'Yes, I think we can do that with a clear conscience, especially since Estelle isn't afraid to make friends with children in a new environment.'

Maryam agreed. She felt the same way. 'Then I'll register her for primary school next year.'

Half a year later, Estelle started school.

Dang had heard about this when he was last at Munny's house with Liam and Nicole, and he immediately had the idea of organising a table at the restaurant for them all to celebrate the occasion. Dang idolised the little girl, who called him Uncle Dang.

Everyone was thrilled with Dang's idea. Only Munny rolled his eyes at the euphoria around him, saying it was too much fuss.

'Just because nobody celebrated when you started school,' said Dang, 'that doesn't mean you have to deprive your daughter of the pleasure.' He poked Munny in the ribs.

Maryam laughed. 'Yes, why not? It would give us an excuse to have lunch together again.'

'Exactly,' Nicole agreed. 'And I could take it as a precedent for our offspring.'

'What?' Maryam exclaimed. 'Don't tell me, you're pregnant?'

All turned their heads questioningly to Nicole and Liam. He took Nicole in his arms, smiled broadly and kissed her on the cheek. 'We only found out for sure a few days ago.'

Nicole beamed.

'Wow, we're flabbergasted, congratulations to you both.' Maryam gave Nicole and Liam a hug.

Munny grinned mischievously at Dang. 'Dude, you need to get a move on. It's not cool to become a dad if you leave it another twenty years. Old fathers aren't good for their children's development.'

Dang just responded with a sidelong glance, making a wry face.

They set a day for the restaurant, about a week before the start of school. Dang busily prepared cupcakes, raspberry hearts and Estelle's favourite food, chicken *amok*, with a view to the party. Munny was glad when the day finally arrived. Dang's preparations in the kitchen were driving him crazy.

Maryam kissed Munny before she went to work, taking the car keys with her. 'Sweetheart, I'll pick up Estelle in the car after work and we'll come straight to the restaurant, okay?'

'Good plan,' said Munny.

Estelle had told them firmly that she absolutely wanted to stay with her old friends at pre-school for as long as possible, which

Maryam was not entirely unhappy about. This allowed her a little more flexibility in her schedule at the newspaper.

'Darling, I can leave the office in about ten minutes and drive straight over to pick up Estelle. I think we can be with you at the restaurant in half an hour, at one o'clock sharp. Guess what? My boss gave Estelle a fancy writing set for her first day at school. Isn't he lovely?' Maryam laughed heartily on the phone.

Munny looked forward to seeing Estelle's face. She would be amazed when she saw the table decorated specially for her!

'Sweetheart, I can't wait to see you,' he said into the phone. 'Dang has decorated the table for her, you wouldn't believe it. It looks like a birthday party.'

Maryam laughed. 'Well, see you in a bit, love you!' she said and hung up.

Munny still had a few preparations to make. Liam helped him with the dessert, which consisted of biscuit letters spelling out 'Estelle' and a strawberry border with ice cream.

Liam put the dessert plates ready in the fridge, so that all that needed to be added later was the ice cream. 'Come on, there's nothing more we can do here. Nicole must be here already.'

They stomped resolutely out of the kitchen.

Nicole, who had just arrived, came beaming into the restaurant and approached Munny. She gave him a very big hug.

'Well now,' he said. 'What brought that on?'

Nicole shook her head. 'Nothing, I'm just happy. I'm wearing looser more comfortable clothes. To prepare for the ... you know.' She winked at him.

Dang rushed into the restaurant. 'Am I too late?' he asked, opening his eyes wide.

'Not yet. Maryam called twenty minutes ago. She's getting Estelle right now. They should be here in about fifteen minutes. But let's have a drink first.'

They sat down at the festive circular table by the window. Nicole complained that Liam had been wrapping her in cotton wool ever since she got pregnant.

Munny looked at his watch. Maryam and Estelle should be arriving soon. Estelle probably needed some time to say goodbye to her pre-school friends. He poured Liam and Dang a glass of French white wine.

They talked about the hotel and Jason's expansion plans. This also affected the restaurants and their kitchens, meaning an increase in staff. For Liam and Munny, this would involve a lot of extra work in the kitchen and the organisation. Munny scratched his head and smiled. 'Who knows, maybe Finn from Raffles in Siem Reap will join us here to take on the management of a new restaurant. I say Liam, that's not a bad idea! He'd fit right in with our team and he's Australian too. Another buddy to surf with, eh Liam?'

Liam gave him a conspiratorial grin.

'Hey, Munny, where's Maryam?' Nicole asked, stroking her belly. 'She's half an hour late now. Me and the bump are getting hungry. Can you give her a call and find out where she is?'

Munny nodded and had the phone to his ear in a second. 'Strange, no connection. Maybe she just arrived at the underground car park.'

They waited.

'Who knows,' said Dang, smirking. 'Munny may have blotted his copybook, and Maryam is standing him up.'

Munny shot Dang a reproachful glance.

'Okay, okay. I'll give her a call, maybe she'll talk to me.' Dang dialled, and then frowned. 'Subscriber temporarily unavailable.'

They none of them knew what to make of it. It wasn't at all like Maryam to go off the radar like this. Munny tried to call her again, but again couldn't get through.

A waitress came out of the kitchen. 'Munny, are we ready to start?'

He looked at her blankly.

Dang waved a hand. 'No, the guests of honour are still missing.'

Munny was torn between mild annoyance at being kept waiting and growing concern. He looked at Dang uneasily.

Dang shrugged. 'Give her another ten minutes.'

Liam and Nicole nodded in agreement.

'Darling, why don't you eat an appetiser at least so that you and the baby have something in your stomachs,' Liam suggested.

Nicole nodded gratefully and did as he suggested.

After what felt like another eternity, Munny called the office. Maryam had left long ago, all apparently according to plan.

He called the pre-school and asked if Estelle was still there. No, she had been picked up half an hour ago by his wife.

Munny was beside himself with worry. They sat broodingly at the table, no one daring to hazard a conjecture. Even Dang was visibly concerned.

Munny jumped up. 'Damn it, I've got to do something. I just can't sit here anymore.' He walked briskly to the exit.

Dang ran after him. 'Munny, where are you going? Stay here. If she's looking for you, she'll come here!'

Liam ran up. 'Come here, Munny, there's someone to see you, the receptionist just told me. They're waiting in the foyer. Let's go, I'll come with you.'

'I'm coming too,' Dang said.

Together with Nicole, they went to the reception. The receptionist indicated a group of three uniformed police officers. As Munny approached, they looked in his direction.

'Are you Oum Munny?' asked one of the men.

Munny swallowed, dry-mouthed. 'Yes, that's me.'

The biggest of the three policemen took off his cap, and the other followed suit.

'Can we sit down over there?' the officer asked.

Munny could only nod. Something must have happened. His gut feeling told him this was bad news.

'I'm the Deputy Commissioner here in Sydney,' the police officer explained as they sat down. He hesitated and looked awkwardly at the floor. 'I'm afraid we have to inform you that your wife has been in a traffic accident.'

Munny jumped up. 'Where is she? My daughter was with her. How are they, what ...'

Liam put his hand on Munny's shoulder. 'Munny, let him finish.'

Nicole and Dang looked shocked. Nicole put her hand over her mouth. 'Oh God ...' she cried softly, with her hand over her mouth and wide-open eyes.

'Yes sir, it's a bad business. What can I say ... A ... a drunk lorry driver coming out of town swerved across the carriageway and collided head-on with your wife's car.'

Munny stood there shocked and could not say anything. A shiver ran down his spine.

Liam looked at the policeman directly. 'Please tell us how they are doing and where they are now.'

The police officer shook his head, troubled, and stared at the ground. His two colleagues also looked down with embarrassment.

'Sir, I am so very sorry to have to tell you that the two people in the car died before help could arrive. First responders tried to help them on the scene ... But your wife and daughter were killed outright ... It's a terrible tragedy. Please take all the time you need. If you can get in touch as soon as you are able to do so, we will take care of the necessary formalities.'

He clumsily produced a card, which Liam took, nodding. 'Thank you, sir. Our deepest condolences, sir.' The three officers nodded solemnly in farewell and left.

Munny still stood there, shaking his head in disbelief. Dang's tears were streaming down his cheeks. Nicole was shaking with violent sobs.

Suddenly Munny let out a tremendous cry. He stood there with his mouth wide open. 'I must go to the hospital and check on them!'

Liam gently took him by the shoulder and pushed him into one of the armchairs. 'Munny, you're in shock, please sit down. Dang, get something to drink.'

Nicole, who had joined them by now and evidently understood what had happened, threw her arms around Munny. 'Oh my God, Munny, this is terrible and beyond words. I can't believe it ... Oh my God.'

Munny was shaken by sobbing fits. 'No, no, no, they should be here ... Why? Why?'

Nicole hugged him and made Munny sit down.

Liam sat down with them and hugged them both, crying.

Suddenly Munny screamed with an unbridled rage and a passion that no one had ever seen from him before: 'This isn't fair, DAMN IT!' He went on cursing, out of control.

Dang pushed him back in his chair and put a glass of water in front of him.

Munny shook his head in despair and looked at Dang with angry apathy. 'Damn! Damn it!' He took the glass of water and hurled it against a pillar opposite the seating area. It shattered loudly into a thousand splinters. Guests looked around in alarm.

Liam touched Munny on the shoulder. 'Munny, we're taking you with us. We have to get out of here. Come on, Dang, you too.'

Liam tried to persuade Munny to leave. But he stood there looking crazed, motionless as a statue. 'I'm not going anywhere. I'm waiting for Maryam and Estelle.'

'Munny, they probably are here,' Nicole said gently, 'but not the way you're thinking. They're with Voramay now.'

'No!!! They're not!' He screamed in agony. Everyone at the front desk looked over at the sad group around the young man whose cries filled the air.

'Come on, Munny, we must get out of here, I can't take any more of this either,' Dang said, tugging at his arm. Munny let himself be led out of the foyer as if in a trance.

When they arrived in the underground car park, he clutched one of the pillars, moaning, and pressed his forehead against it. He screamed his pain out again and again. The echo screamed back relentlessly. Liam's jeep drove up, and Dang bundled him in. Nicole got in silently in front.

Liam had a hard time concentrating in the heavy traffic. The other drivers kept hooting at him. He shook his head in disbelief. He glanced at Dang in the rearview mirror. Dang just shook his head in shock and put his arm around Munny, who was looking out of the window apathetically. Nicole, in the front passenger seat, was crying quietly to herself. Liam put his hand over to comfort her while driving and held hers tightly.

When they got home, Nicole made up a guest bed for Munny. 'We have to watch Munny very carefully now. I don't know what he might be capable of.' Dang and Liam nodded in agreement. 'Yeah, we have to look after him,' Liam murmured as he went into the kitchen.

The next morning, Liam showed Dang into the kitchen and indicated with a nod the empty whisky bottle lying on the floor. Dang shook his head sadly. Munny was still in bed, sleeping it off.

Liam, Nicole and Dang were sitting around the kitchen island, coffee cups to hand. None of them felt like having breakfast. Nicole sipped at her tea, red-eyed.

Liam looked at Dang questioningly. 'Should just the two of us go to the police station? Maybe we can spare him the hard part. Nicole could stay here with him.'

Dang nodded. 'Yes, we can do that. But if he has to go to the morgue, he has to do it in person. We'll just have to go with him.'

Early that afternoon, Munny crawled out of bed, eyes swollen like after a boxing match, and reached for a fresh bottle of bourbon instead of the coffee cup.

Liam took it from him.

'Damn it, you're not my nanny, leave me alone. This is my damn shitty life. I was found in the dirt and that's how I'll end up,' Munny slurred angrily.

'Come on, here's your coffee. Drink that first, it'll help you feel better.' Dang pushed the cup over to him.

'I'm going back to bed anyway. I can't stand the daylight.' He turned around and made as if to go back to bed.

Liam took him by both shoulders. 'Munny, I'm sorry, but we still have some bureaucratic stuff to do today. Dang and I will accompany you. You need to shower and shave now, then we'll go together.'

'Like hell I do, can you please just get off my back!' The other two stood there in shock. This was not the Munny they knew. And no wonder. Munny felt a thick swelling around his eyes, the corners of his mouth were fixed and downturned. Seeing the faces of his friends, it was clear to him what a sight he made.

Munny allowed Liam and Dang to accompany him for the identification. When he saw the unharmed but lifeless faces of his wife and daughter, he broke down sobbing. Paramedics carried him out on a stretcher, his eyes wide open, staring at the ceiling. In the hallway, he let out a heart-wrenching cry of pain.

On the drive back, Dang sat with him in the back seat and held his hand.

Later on, Munny sat in apathetic silence on the sofa, barely paying attention to his friends.

'We'll give him a few more days,' Liam decided resolutely.

For Munny, the words were far away.

'Nicole wants to help organise the funeral,' Liam continued. 'After that, he has to come to work. Something to do and a change of scenery are what he needs right now.'

X. SAMSARA:
THE WHEEL OF LIFE

Work kept Munny going, but the funeral pushed him back into his lethargy and lack of motivation. Maryam's boss and the whole department came, as did all the kitchen staff and some mothers whose children had been friends with Estelle. Despite their sympathetic support, having all these people around him reopened his wounds.

'I need some fresh air,' he murmured to himself and slipped away from the mourners' lunch table to leave the building.

He leaned against the wall of the house for half an hour before Liam finally found him. Tears were running down his cheeks, and he was holding a bottle of whisky.

'God damn it, Munny, you must stop this drinking. It won't bring anyone back to life,' Liam hissed at him angrily. He snatched the liquor from his hand, and led him, listless and a bit unsteady, back to the table. The others exchanged meaningful glances.

'I think it's better if he lies down after all that,' said Nicole. 'Let's go.'

Many days later when Munny was finally able to live alone in his apartment again, he showed up in the kitchen of the hotel restaurant. Everyone greeted him with obvious relief and made a visible effort to make him feel part of the family.

Munny lost track of the work processes, and kept asking what preparations had already been made. It seemed as if he had lost interest in what had once been his passion. Liam had obviously noticed it. 'Dang, listen, I'm not just worried about Munny's current state, I'm also concerned about our kitchen. More specifically, about the high level of our kitchen. With his current lack of concentration, it's a worry. We'll both have to see how we can deal with this unobtrusively until he gets a grip on himself again. Agreed?'

Almost with indifference, Munny noticed how Dang instructed his team to be more disciplined in their preparations. Dang too had observed that Munny was erratic and often distracted at work.

Since Nicole and Liam's daughter was due to arrive soon, Liam asked Dang to keep an eye on Munny.

Dang had a lot of ideas for taking care of his friend. He tried to persuade him to go surfing or hiking in the Saddleback Mountains, but without much success. The only place Munny would go with him was the pub. Dang almost felt guilty about accompanying him there as he was afraid that his recently acquired alcoholic tendencies would lead to trouble. But he thought it was better to be with Munny than to know that he was alone in the bar. However, it was always a hassle and a test of patience before he could get Munny to leave.

Munny had become a regular at a few bars in the Kings Cross neighbourhood. Some were dingy and seedy and were frequented by the clientele of the red-light district. Evidently Munny, at other times so concerned with aesthetics, was no longer bothered. Quite the contrary. In such places he felt unobtrusive, and the bartender already knew his preferences from his frequent visits: only whisky and vodka.

On one of these evenings when he didn't go home until long

after he'd finished work, he was standing alone, swaying, against the wall of the dimly lit bar and watching the world go by.

It was packed on this Thursday evening with lots of wild down-and-out characters hanging around. There were probably also a few surfers there, drawn by the low prices. Munny knew that even the bartender was a surfer. He earned his money in the bar to finance his hobby. Others were probably truck drivers from the mines in the outback.

A surfer approached Munny. 'Hi mate, I'm going to the bar, can I get you a refill?'

Munny nodded expressionlessly. The man left and returned a few minutes later with two glasses of whisky. 'The barman told me that's what you always drink. You from around here?'

Munny nodded and looked at the blond guy with his dishevelled hair and sun-tanned face. He had a broad, winning smile and radiated the kind of casual coolness that Munny had always admired in others.

'You've probably seen better days, eh?' The guy grinned at him. 'Man, you should go to a decent beach party again to get your groove back. By the way, my name's Damon, I live in a caravan on Bondi Beach. You fancy dropping by sometime? If you surf too, that'd be really cool. We're a pretty fun bunch there.'

Munny nodded and looked sideways at Damon, who was wearing a washed-out, denim-blue T-shirt.

'There's a full moon party coming up tomorrow. Come and join us! You'll find us on the beach in front of the Backpackers Inn. A mate of mine runs it. There's always something to drink, as well as snacks. Okay, man?' Damon gave Munny a friendly pat on the shoulder and shook him lightly.

Munny nodded. 'Oh, I'm Munny ... uh ... okay, I'll see you tomorrow,' he mumbled.

Damon grinned. 'Good. Now I've got errands to run. I'll see you then.'

The next day, Munny was a full hour and a half late for work.

Liam glared at him. 'God damn it, Munny, get it together. Just look at you. Always these puffy eyes and bad breath. I can't work with you like this. You have a responsibility to your team. Do you think they don't notice when you're not pulling your weight?' Liam threw a towel into a corner of the kitchen in exasperation.

Munny looked at Liam with a glassy stare. 'Sorry.' He turned around with drooping shoulders and focused on his preparations. Liam watched him with a thoughtful expression. Dang nodded to him – 'Don't worry, I'll deal with it.'

Moments later, Dang stood next to Munny. 'What are you doing after work today?'

'I'm going to Bondi Beach for a full moon party. A surfer invited me last night. Why don't you come?'

Dang nodded slowly, looking surprised. 'Do you know these guys?'

'Nope, only one of them, Damon. Come on, let's go and have a few beers with them.'

Dang nodded hesitantly. 'All right, but I'm driving.'

When they arrived at Bondi Beach, laughter, music and the buzz of voices could already be heard in the distance. They followed the sound to the beach and looked around. A casual crowd of some forty people were standing scattered about on the sand, drinks in hand. Most were aged between twenty and thirty-five, Munny estimated. There was a boisterous atmosphere. Some girls in bikinis danced laughingly with surfers to the metallic music that blared from a ghetto blaster. As they walked through the crowd, Damon appeared behind them. 'Cool man, glad you came, Munny.'

Munny indicated Dang with a nod. 'This is my friend Dang. We work together.'

'Okay, get yourselves a beer over there. My buddy Dan from the Inn has some burgers on the grill. Get what you need. You'll find me in front with the others.'

'Well, what do you think of the gig?' Munny wanted to know.

Dang nodded cautiously. 'Well, cool location. These guys here seem to have nothing else to do but surf. Do they all live here at the Inn? What else do they do, and how do they make a living?'

'Man, you've become completely bourgeois. I don't care what else they do. This looks like fun, and I need that now.' Munny walked off with a beer in his hand to a group of girls, leaving the stunned Dang standing.

The surfer community was definitely good for Munny. He laughed freely again for the first time.

Later, Dang and Munny were standing with Damon in a group of somewhat wild-looking surfers who immediately made the two newcomers feel at ease. Damon put his arm around Munny's shoulder. 'I like you better today than I did yesterday in the bar. Come with me, I've got a few pick-me-ups in case you're feeling down again.'

He led Munny away from the group to his caravan, which was standing in the car park of the Inn. 'What you probably need for your … depression … is this.' He laughed as if he had made a good joke. 'It's good stuff to smoke. You'll feel better in a minute, and the surfing comes easy after that. Have a go and take a puff.' He offered Munny a hand-rolled cigarette. Munny looked at him for a long time. 'Actually, I don't smoke.'

'Man, a few puffs won't hurt you, and besides, it's a full moon tonight, you have to go with the flow.' He shoved Munny with his shoulder.

'Well, you're right. I do need a pick-me-up. Give it here.' Munny took the cigarette from Damon.

'It's prime stuff, go ahead. A lot of people here take it.'

Munny sat down on the steps of the caravan next to Damon. They smoked a joint together.

'So, how is it?' Damon asked, amused.

Munny grinned. 'I feel a bit dizzy, but it's good for the mood.'

Damon nodded. 'You can come back anytime if you need anything. I always have something in reserve. The others here do the same. Here, take one for later.' He pushed another joint behind Munny's ear. 'Come on, the party is really taking off now. Let's join the girls.'

The crowd on the beach seemed to have doubled and was now a really big throng of exuberant people.

As Munny and Damon mingled with the crowd again, Dang approached Munny. 'I thought you'd abandoned me here with all these girls. Where did you get to?'

'Oh, Damon was showing me his caravan.'

Dang shook his head with amusement. 'It must be a pretty big trailer, the time you took.'

Munny put his arm around Dang's shoulder and led him back to the group. 'Come on, let's dance.'

Dang looked taken aback.

'What's up? Come on, let's have some fun, Dang. Or do you want to mope around?'

'It's cool that you're more yourself again,' said Dang. 'I'm just surprised. I haven't seen you laugh in a long time.'

Munny paid no attention. He was looking with interest at the females in the party. He headed for a dark-haired European woman who returned his smile at once. Sandra was Italian and told them that she was taking a year off from her studies.

They drank and partied until the early morning.

'Come on, let's think about going, I can't do any more.' Dang tried to pull Munny up out of the sand. 'What for?' his friend slurred. 'It's cool here. Stay a bit longer.'

Dang shook his head. 'Nah, I need to go to bed now and so do you.'

Munny shook his head with abandon. 'Nah, I'm not going yet. Tomorrow is a day off, no work. Treat yourself for a change.'

'Come on, Munny, call it a night. You've had enough for now. I'll drive you home.' Dang was getting impatient.
Munny shook his head stubbornly, still holding Sandra. 'Now that things are getting really cosy here? Can't you see I've got my Italian girl here? You're a real killjoy, leave me alone,' he mumbled.

'Damn it all,' Dang shouted. 'Do you have to crash and burn every time? I don't want you getting wasted again. I'm your friend, remember!'

'Oh, fuck it,' said Munny. Laughing, he lay back on the sand with the woman in his arms and she giggled in response.

Dang stomped away angrily towards the car park.

A little way away from the party people, Munny lay with the girl in front of a small sand dune. They smoked Damon's second joint together.

In the darkness, he slid his hands under her shirt. Her soft full breasts encouraged him to do more. His blood rushed to his ears. He took off her T-shirt and shorts along with her panties and pulled her close. She explored his naked body with her hands. He lay down on top of her, impatiently pushed her legs apart and kissed her hard nipples.

She embraced him wildly, audibly inhaling. He groaned roughly and made the most of it. He hadn't had sex for a long time and took her greedily several more times, giving his lust free rein. She seemed to enjoy it too and they rolled over each other again and again, panting and moaning.

Only when the first light of dawn appeared did they let go of each other, exhausted, and fell asleep as they were.

A hand on his shoulder shook him awake.

'Man, you really went all out.'

Munny blinked as he looked into Damon's grinning face.

He nodded in the direction of the naked Italian girl, who was still asleep. 'Better go and put some clothes on before the beach patrol arrive. And your chick here too. I'll be in the caravan making coffee. Come and join me.'

Munny felt as if his head were splitting. Everything was spinning, and the beach and the sea seemed to merge into one. He was overcome by a feeling of intense thirst and his mouth felt parched. What had actually happened last night? Where was Dang? He tried desperately to piece together his memories. The Italian girl, Sandra, came to and smiled confidently at him.

'Great night that was, we can do it again anytime.' Dressed again in full gear, she straddled him and gave him a kiss.

'Say, do you know where my friend Dang got to?'

She laughed. 'Yeah, you probably scared him off yesterday when he wanted to drive you home. I think he left.'

Munny sat up and took his face in both hands, groaning. 'Shit, I didn't mean to do that. I have to call him. But first I'm going to Damon's for a coffee. You coming?'

'No, *caro mio*, I have to work, otherwise they won't let me stay in Australia ... you know, work and travel and all that.' Sandra stood up and waved goodbye. 'See you again sometime. Damon has my number. Ask him if you want to meet up with me. *Ciao*!'

Munny tried to shake himself awake. 'My God, what happened here?' he muttered to himself.

In the caravan, he collapsed into a chair. 'I think I could do with a strong coffee.'

'Yeah, that's my impression too,' Damon said, patting Munny appreciatively on the upper arm. 'Man, I wouldn't have expected that. You've got a few tricks up your sleeve, haven't you?'

Munny looked away sheepishly. 'I shouldn't have started smoking in the first place.'

'Come on, but the party was fun. And everything that came afterwards, too, surely.' Damon slapped his thigh and laughed.

'I have to apologise to my friend Dang first. I must have pissed him off pretty badly yesterday when I was drunk.'

'Nonsense, he'll come around. Stay here and we'll go surfing. It's your day off!'

Nevertheless, Munny tried to reach Dang. No success. Dang didn't pick up, which he always did when he saw his number. Munny shrugged his shoulders. 'All right, then we'll go surfing.'

Late that afternoon, Damon offered to drive Munny into town. 'Why don't you come by our favourite bar for a beer tonight? Some of the guys from yesterday will be there, too.'

Damon was already engaged in conversation with a man at the bar. When he saw Munny arrive, he waved him over and introduced him to his friend. 'He keeps getting me stuff and I sell it on. It's good business. You should try it sometime.'

'No thanks, I've already got a job,' Munny said and laughed.

Damon raised his eyebrows meaningfully. 'Look, I've got some super-pure stuff here, cocaine, just bought it. You've got to try it. I can do you a line. It's a real mood-lifter, in case your surroundings are getting on your nerves again.'

Munny shook his head. 'Nah, forget it, the joints yesterday already hit me pretty hard. Thanks.'

He said goodbye after two drinks and walked home.

The next morning Munny ran into Dang, who had apparently been in the kitchen very early on preparing for a gala event.

'Listen Dang, I'm really sorry about what happened. To be honest, I don't remember anything. I just know you were pissed off.'

'Oh, fuck off ...', Dang snapped at him with a nasty look. Munny's jaw dropped. He had never seen Dang so angry.

'My God, what happened, what did I say?' He looked at Dang with wide, questioning eyes.

'Man, you idiot, are you telling me you don't remember what you said? YOU told me that YOU don't give a *shit* about our friendship!' Dang deliberately dragged out the obscenity.

Munny gasped for breath. 'What? Did I really say that? Oh man, you're right, I'm an idiot. Man, Dang, I'm really fucking sorry, shit!'

Dang shook his head at him. 'You should be more careful how you choose your words. You already sound like those dope-heads at the party. You should avoid their company in future, it's not good for you. Now let me work, and just do your job properly for a change.'

Munny turned away, crestfallen, and absentmindedly went back to his preparations. He really couldn't remember much about the beach party. Damn, had it been the joints? He worked on with Dang, taciturn and unmotivated.

When Liam joined them in the kitchen, he gave Dang a questioning look. Dang just shook his head and furrowed his brow. The mood in the kitchen was tense and taciturn.

Frustrated after a long day, Munny took off his work clothes. He didn't know where to go. He usually went out for a meal with Dang. Only now did he realise how much he missed his friend.

He decided to go to a bar for a drink. What the heck, better alone in a good mood than to have the company of a party pooper.

Well loaded after a few hours in the first bar, he arrived at his dimly lit local when it was already late. It was not too busy today. Just as he was getting ready to leave, Damon put a hand on his shoulder.

'Good to see you, Munny. So, did you and your buddy patch things up?'

Munny shook his head, depressed.

'Man, what a tight-ass. He doesn't want you to have a good time. Come on, let's get ourselves a proper drink.'

Grateful to have someone to talk to, he followed Damon to the bar. They had a double whisky. Then another.

'Man, you're not getting into the mood tonight. But it was different last time. Should I call Sandra?' He shoved Munny in a friendly way. Munny just shook his head in frustration.

'Not feeling good? You should do something about that. I've got what you need.'

Munny shook his head again and declined, slightly slurring his words.

'Come on, give it a try. I'll let you have the first one for free. You'll see, a small line like that goes down well. Just come with me to the table in the corner at the back. I'm going to have a little something myself. It's been a hard day.'

Munny let himself be drawn along. He was swaying, with his third whisky in his hand.

Damon deftly showed him how to snort a line of cocaine. 'Now you. A little less to start with. Here, go ahead.'

Munny snorted up the line. A hellish sting shot through his nose. It felt like it continued up to his eye. Munny opened both eyes wide and shook himself. Damon laughed. 'Well, that wasn't so hard. Drink something, then you'll be in a better mood faster.'

Everything in Munny's head went like cotton wool. After just a few minutes he felt light as a feather. Damon grinned broadly, drawing Munny under his spell. They laughed together with no inhibitions.

'You know, Damon, I'm actually married to Maryam,' Munny explained. 'Buuuut she left me ... uh, by the way, don't tell her about ... about ... the affair with Sandra. Maryam will never come baaaack ... you know?'

Both laughed uproariously, and Damon promised sincerely not to tell Maryam – they were friends, after all.

The next morning, Munny had no idea how he had got home. A glance at the clock made him jump in fright. He was already over an hour late. Without showering, he ran to the hotel restaurant.

Liam gave him a dirty look. 'Have you seen yourself in the mirror lately? You look like death warmed up. And it doesn't smell like you've had a shower either. Damn it, Munny, get your act together!'

Liam had never spoken to him so harshly. That was all he needed! First Dang, and now Liam was mad at him too.

His nose was itching like crazy. He kept sniffing and rubbing it. The only good thing about Damon's stuff was that he was wide awake and concentrated.

If it helped him to get back to his old efficiency, a small dose from time to time might not be a bad idea.

The next few days, Munny came on time and worked like a machine. He bought more of the stuff from Damon and took it in small amounts every evening at home, together with a double whisky.

The rift between Liam, Dang and him had smoothed out to some extent, but there was still a slight breach between them. They were polite to each other, laughed at times, but it just was not the same as it used to be.

Munny held out a sweet spicy sauce for Dang to try with a Wagyu beef steak. 'Here, try it, is it too spicy, or do you like it?'

Dang tilted his head, considering. 'Well, you used to add a smoky note. I think that's what's missing here. I would take out some of the spice, not every guest likes that.'

Munny nodded appreciatively. 'Thanks, Dang.'

Liam heard that Munny needed more and more feedback on the flavours he created.

Everyone in the kitchen team was talking about how Munny's taste explosions were losing their power. Munny showed little imagination. Sometimes he oversalted the dishes in the seasoning phase, or some ingredient got left out.

One evening, Liam had had enough of this, and took him aside for a serious talk. 'Tell me, Munny, what has happened to your usual sensitive and ingenious fine-tuning? What you are doing now is average, and doesn't match the style and level of our restaurant.'

Munny shrugged helplessly. 'I'm not sure what you mean. What do you want me to do?'

Liam looked at him in amazement. The old Munny would never have shown himself so helpless. He would always have come up with a surprising culinary solution in a flash. 'What's going on with you? You've become so, so ... different since Maryam and Estelle died. If there's anything we can do to help you cope with the loss, just say the word, but don't bottle it up, okay? You've changed so much and lost so much weight. You don't laugh like you used to. We haven't gone surfing in a long time. You turn down invitations and go off the radar. I say again, Munny, you have to talk to us, we want to help you. Dang says he doesn't know what to do with you either. He just told me he doesn't like your new so-called friends. Do me a favour and do something about it!'

Munny looked at him in amazement, almost hollow-eyed. 'Sorry if it wasn't up to scratch today.' He stuck his nose in the air and slouched away.

Dang approached Munny during a break. 'There's a Champions League game on live TV tonight. Shall we watch it at your place?'

Munny nodded. 'Yeah, okay. Bring something to eat.'

As they watched the game over nachos, dips, and beer, it was almost like old times between them. Dang made suggestive remarks, they laughed a lot, and stuffed themselves full of junk food.

During a break in the game, Dang went to the bathroom. Shortly after, he shot out again, his eyes sparkling with anger. He grabbed Munny, who was lying on the sofa, by the front of his T-shirt and pulled him up abruptly. He held a small mirror with white powder residue right under Munny's nose. 'WHAT is this?' he shouted at Munny. 'Is it what I think it is?? Have you completely lost your mind? Is that why you're constantly rubbing your nose and your sense of taste is going down the drain? You idiot! Aren't you already in deep enough shit? Man, you're a crackhead! Are you crazy! You can get fired in our line of work for something like that!' Dang's neck veins visibly swelled.

Getting himself under control with an effort, he addressed Munny in a calmer voice. 'Damn it, don't ruin your life and destroy our friendship and your hard-won success by doing drugs. Is it that Damon who sold you the stuff?'

Munny tugged at his hair in annoyance and furrowed his brow. 'Man, it's only small amounts. It makes me much more alert and focused. It's not that big a deal. Leave me and my life alone. Enough has happened already. I don't want you interfering in what little life I have left. GODDAMN IT! IT'S MY LIFE AFTER ALL!'

Dang came very close and looked him in the eye. 'I'll tell you your prospects, buddy. If Liam finds out about this, he'll have no choice but to kick you off the team. You'll end up on the street, and you won't get a job in that state. Your fabulous friends won't give you a roof over your head without money and will drop you. I'm warning you. Don't throw away everything you've achieved! I won't say a word to anyone, I'll cover for you. But you have to make changes urgently and come off the stuff.'

'Damn it, I'm not an addict! I need the stuff at the moment to reduce stress. You'd better keep your good advice to yourself. It would be best if you changed something in your own life and found yourself a woman.' Munny raised his voice. 'Then you can get off on lecturing her. I guess there's a reason why no woman ever wanted you yet!'

Dang's face turned pale and sad. 'Munny, I've tried hard, but that's the end of our long friendship. I don't have to let myself be insulted by a junkie in this way.' He got up silently and, without turning around, pulled the apartment door closed behind him.

Munny's ears were buzzing with tension. He could hear his blood pressure rushing, his heart pounding like a sledgehammer. How could he change anything about his situation? Maryam and Estelle would never come back to him, with or without drugs.

His life was ruined, he thought, feeling hurt and bitter inside. He shrugged his shoulders, picked up the mirror that Dang had thrown on the floor and went into the bathroom. He took a significantly higher dose than usual. He just wanted to forget and numb the pain.

He lay down on the sofa with a glass of whisky. The TV was still on. The background noise was welcome. It made him feel less alone.

His dreams wandered back to old times. But every single dream always ended in chaos. In every dream, it all fell apart. He had fought it again and again, without the least success.

The next working day he overslept completely. When he surfaced in the evening, confused and thirsty, and peered at his phone, he saw that Liam had tried to reach him several times. He bit his lower lip. Damn, since yesterday afternoon!

When he rejoined his team after two days' absence, Liam intercepted him at the door. 'We need to talk.' He pulled him ungently into an adjoining room, making an angry face. 'It's an unparalleled lack of respect for your team. Dang is also bottling things up and won't tell me what's going on with you. I'm giving you an ultimatum. If it happens again, you're out of here. And if it turns out that you're not just an alcoholic, but also dependent on something else, I'll have to tell Jason. That's definitely a no-go for our hotel.'

Munny looked at Liam, unmoved and hollow-eyed. 'Got it, man. Sorry. I wasn't at my best.'

'Munny, do you understand the gravity of the situation?'

'Yeah, yeah.' Munny slipped out quietly and headed for the kitchen.

That same evening, Munny went back to his local bar and got drunk again. As he was staggering out, his legs gave way and he ended up lying on the street across the road from the bar.

Later on, in the middle of the night, he saw Dang's face above him.

'I'll take you home. The barman called me, after he realised you were in a bad way. You're drunk as a skunk and can't seem to control yourself or your life anymore.'

Later, in Munny's apartment, he let Mummy drop into bed. 'You have to get out of this nightmare. Get help from a professional.

This has nothing to do with having a drink or a joint occasionally. You're a drug addict. Damn it, don't be so stubborn – just let yourself be helped and listen to your friends!'

Munny shook his head stoically. 'Man, I don't need any help. I'm a grownup. I just had a little too much to drink. Will you please stop bugging me about it?'

Dang went to work the next morning and excused Munny to Liam, who rolled his eyes in exasperation. Then he called Munny. 'You're let off for today. And Munny, please consider going to rehab. You might just get your old life back.'

Munny laughed bitterly. 'My old life? I'll tell you where my old life is. Just go to Rookwood General Cemetery. That's where my old life is, in two graves side by side, four metres down!'

It was definitely no good talking to Munny about this. A great sadness, and a sense of finality, came over Dang.

The next day, Munny still hadn't shown up for work. Dang talked to Liam. He told him what had been going on, and about the drug scene of which Munny was a part.

Liam was shocked. Despite his vivid imagination, he hadn't thought it could be so bad. Dang asked Liam to wait before sacking him and to give him one last chance.

Munny turned up at the restaurant after several days with a significant amount of alcohol in his blood. Liam took him by the arm and pulled him into the still empty restaurant.

'I have given you another chance again and again, but you haven't taken it. This is the end. I have to hand you your red card. Your cooking has gone completely to the dogs and is no longer up to our standards. You've got to go! If you want, Jason will tell you in person. But I actually wanted to spare you the embarrassment of appearing before him in this state. Before the man who, like all of us here, welcomed you with open arms! You can vacate the apartment by the end of the month. That's enough time for you to find a new one. You'll hand in the keys at the front desk and get your documents, along with a favourable reference. Do you understand?'

Munny waved him off, swaying. 'I don't care. I've done so much for this place, and this is how you thank me? Screw the place, screw your friendship!' His pride deeply wounded, he lurched through the staff door and out into the open. Everyone had abandoned him.

XI. THE OTHER LIFE

Thanks to Damon, he found a shabby one-room apartment in the red-light district near Kings Cross. He slept off his alcohol and drug consumption during the day and became active at night.

'Say, Damon, you suggested a job to me a while back, right? Is it still on?'

Damon grinned. 'Yeah, sure, buddy. You can help me deliver the goods and collect the money. I'll tell you how to do it.'

Munny soon worked out which customers were best reached where, who was well off, who checked exactly what they got and how much they paid for it. Some were very unpleasant, choleric lads, quick to fly into a rage and start a fight; some were just happy when the deal was done, and they could make off with the stuff. Munny preferred the latter sort.

Increasingly, he diverted some of the deliveries to Damon's customers for his own use. As a result of his drug intake, there was nothing left of his desire to eat well and discover new things. He lost a lot of weight and, with his wiry upper arms and sunken chest, looked years older. His high cheekbones stood out in his gaunt face.

Because of his constant need for money to buy drugs, he discovered gambling and got caught up in ever-increasing debts. He often played poker or roulette for hours and days without eating. In the beginning, he had a fair amount of success at poker, which encouraged him to bet larger and larger sums.

One evening, he had been standing at the roulette table in the casino for a good hour. Things were going swimmingly for him. One win followed hot on the heels of another. Increasing murmurs were heard coming from the crowd of onlookers around the table, who were eagerly following his progress. This further fuelled his elation. Munny stood, as if hypnotised by a snake, in front of the roulette wheel, watching the ball. Another hit!

He breathed out tensely. Really he should take his winnings and leave now. He had already won more than twice his entire savings that evening. He shouldn't push his luck any longer. The crowd around him noticed his hesitation and cheered him on to keep playing. He pursed his lips. Well, just one more time and then off to the bar! He placed his entire winnings on red. That was less of a risk than on a number or a combination.

With sweat on his forehead, he watched the ball intently. Was it still circling? Come on, just one last turn! The wheel slowed down. The ball jumped up – red! He cheered inwardly and the crowd screamed.

But it wasn't over. The ball was catapulted out of the slot by its own momentum and popped into another one. Black!

Blackness descended on Munny, as black as the square the ball landed on. The crowd screamed. Some covered their mouths in shock. Munny perceived everything as if in a trance. He only saw the croupier's rake slide all the chips he had won into the drop slot. When asked if he wanted to continue playing, he just shook his head ever so slightly and slunk away from the table like a beaten dog. What an idiot he was!

Well, better luck next time, he said to himself, some time and three drinks later. He urgently needed to make up for his lack of money. He had to repay old debts in time, before one of the weirdos he had to do with came after him.

He tried to borrow money to pay the rent for the shabby apartment and to finance his ever increasing drug use.

Damon's customers were complaining more and more often that the packages did not contain the promised quantities. Very serious threats soon reached Damon and Munny. Brutal guys showed up at Damon's apartment and threatened him.

Damon confronted Munny about it, standing over him menacingly. 'Do you have any idea, in your pitiful brain, how much it costs me to keep these people off my back?' he shouted in his face. 'You pull this kind of shit here and saddle me with thugs I have to appease and bribe just to make them go away! You can pay me back the money down to the last cent, along with the bribe I had to pay so that the bosses don't find out that someone on my team has had a hand in the till. You can also replace the stuff you've stolen from me. I don't care how you do it. After all, I have a reputation to lose. Do you understand me?'

Munny saw that Damon's face was contorted into a grimace of rage. He smelled his bad breath. Damon's saliva drops stuck to his face.

'You'll pay me back within a week. Is that understood? Until you get the money together, I'll pay back the damages to my customers. You better get off your ass. I'll hand you over to the bosses' goons without blinking an eye. I don't give a shit what they do to you. Consider this week an interest-free loan from me to you.'

Munny nodded, intimidated, and promised to pay back the money in small amounts. He would also do a few favours for Damon, he said, which would count towards his debt.

Among other things, Damon gave him the task of 'procuring' the outstanding money from a defaulting small-time drug dealer's apartment.

Munny had no experience at all in this kind of thing, and approached the business rashly and unprepared. He was promptly caught searching the apartment. The very much bulkier, heavily tattooed dealer and a friend of his beat him up badly in the apartment and then dropped him out of a car, leaving him unconscious in a back alley, covered in blood and surrounded by plastic bags and cardboard boxes.

When Damon missed Munny's next instalment payment and Munny didn't answer his phone or show up at his place, he went looking for him, furious.

After a short search and a tip from his guys, Damon found Munny whimpering on the ground in a dark alley. Damon still had Dang's number, which Munny had given him in better times. 'I just found your buddy Munny in a courtyard. He's lucky I found him. He owes me a lot of money and others too. They're probably responsible for the state he's in. Best thing would be if you bring the money here, and then you can pick up your friend, or what's left of him – otherwise I'll leave him here till he rots. Do you understand? Yes?'

'What has he done?'

'Enough. He also has a lot of gambling debts, incidentally, which I paid for him. He still owes my customers money too, because he kept diverting stuff from their goods. If you don't want their bonzos settling your bosom buddy's account, you'd better pay up before I change my mind and tell them where you live. Wouldn't that be inconvenient for you and your reputation at work?' Damon laughed throatily.

'How much?' Dang asked.

The next day, Dang paid off all Munny's debts to Damon, who took the money with a mean grin.

He looked after Munny at his apartment for days and got him medication. He avoided talking to Liam about it at all costs. Liam would have called him crazy since he considered Munny's condition beyond hope.

When Munny was able to talk again, Dang explained to him what had happened. Munny cried silently to himself. Dang felt deeply sorry for his friend, who had fallen so low, and was shivering and trembling. With an emaciated face, Munny begged Dang through tears to get him drugs from somewhere, which Dang categorically refused to do.

XII. OUTBACK

Dang took great care of Munny and tried to foster their old friendship. Seven days later when he came home from work, he found a crumpled piece of paper with Munny's handwriting on it, torn out of a notebook. It was crabbed and awkward and lacking in elegance, like his new life.

'My dear friend Dang, I know what you have done for me. I am endlessly grateful for your loyal friendship and your endless patience but I can't find the right words to beg your forgiveness for the last few months and what happened.

'I don't want to go on being a burden to you. You've already done more than enough. Dang, I'm so sorry for all the things I've said to you. It was this terrible uncontrollable rage inside me and anger about my life. None of that has anything to do with you. Please forgive all the harsh words! Please remember our good times together and forget all the other crap. I will turn my back on Sydney for good. Too many painful memories. Yours Munny.' His signature was smudged by water stains and barely legible.

Dang's eyes welled up until tears cascaded down his cheeks. So it was a farewell letter! Fear crept up his arms, paralysing him. He hoped his friend wouldn't do himself any harm.

In panic, he searched the relevant neighbourhoods for Munny, but his friend had disappeared from the face of the earth. He couldn't discover any sign of him. His phone was evidently disconnected because of the many unpaid bills. Reluctantly, he called Damon. But Munny hadn't contacted him either. Nor had he been seen in his local for some time.

'Good luck, Munny,' whispered Dang.

Before leaving the apartment, Munny had stocked up on food and a few fresh clothes from Dang. He had heard that a full moon party was going to be held at Bondi Beach again and that Damon wanted to make preparations for the catering on site. He presumed that he would be on the road in his VW bus as early as lunchtime.

So the coast should be clear. He knew his way around Damon's apartment by now, and knew where to look for the stuff. He crept cautiously through an unlocked metal door in the back yard to reach the apartment. The key to it was in its familiar hiding place. Damon was so afraid of being caught in the act during one of his deals that he always kept a 'security key' in readiness, so he could get out quickly and unobtrusively, taking the cash with him. Munny grinned to himself when he found everything still in the old place. As his find showed, Damon had hardly expected he would dare to break into the apartment, otherwise he would have hidden things somewhere else. Luck was finally on Munny's side!

Carrying a sports bag with all the drugs and the wads of cash together with Damon's sneakers, he silently crept out of the apartment onto the street behind. This time he kept a keen lookout. He didn't want to mess up now, like with his last failed break-in. A bizarre sense of satisfaction came over him.

He used the back roads to avoid meeting anyone. No risk-taking. If Damon found him now, he would probably not survive it.

After a few hours, he left the city heading north. He managed to hitchhike, mostly on the back of trucks. A few farmers also gave him a lift for short distances.

A warm feeling of happiness spread through him. He felt so incredibly free. Free from responsibility. Free from any predetermined daily routine. Free from the pressure of having to justify himself.

He decided to sign on as a labourer on farms to get a place to stay and, for the time being, a roof over his head. A trucker told him that there were many cattle stations and mines a few hundred miles north near Cobar where he could find work.

Munny decided to make his way there over the next few weeks. He didn't think anyone would be looking for him in that part of the world.

He took a job on a sheep farm on the way to Cobar for starvation wages. Deep down, he was glad to be part of a group again. The only thing that made him very uncomfortable and weighed on his mind was the thought of the communal accommodation for workers on the farm. He dreaded not having a proper place of his own to retreat to. There was no obvious alternative. But where could he hide the money and Damon's drugs? Where could he shoot up without being noticed? He had to find solutions to these problems as quickly as possible.

He found a way to slip inconspicuously into the communal showers or toilets during work breaks. The shot helped him get through the day without breaking down at work or showing signs of exhaustion. Every evening, he retreated to one of the stables for a cigarette. He found times when these were empty so that he could inject himself undisturbed. He thought to ask if he could exchange his wages for the farmer's motorhome. Though dented and practically ready to be scrapped, it was still roadworthy but just sitting around unused.

The farmer grinned, shaking his head in disbelief. 'All right then, you can have the old rust bucket. I'll deduct half of your wages. Consider it an advance.' He sucked on his cigar butt. 'Just put it over there, way past the sheep fences. And don't even think about parking that old junk in my yard again, I'll be glad to see the last of it.' He eyed Munny with narrowed eyes.

After cleaning and clearing out the vehicle, Munny was able to lie down on his improvised bed – a horsehair mattress from the attic of the farmhouse – two nights later. He fell asleep contentedly after his daily work, but was haunted by crazy dreams.

He took great care to hide everything – including Damon's cash and the drugs – in a cavity in the underside of the caravan.

He kept a low profile and spoke little to the other workers. He cleaned out stables and provided transport services. All without responding to the various attempts at contact from the other employees. He realised that with his emaciated and haggard face, which he hid behind stubble, and his shoulder-length hair, he was generally regarded as an oddball – as someone who was not quite up to life's challenges.

Fortunately the farmer never asked him about his past. He received his pay in cash every week. Nevertheless, he kept a watchful eye on the others, among whom, he judged – based on his experience of the drug scene – there were some dangerous types who should not be underestimated, probably just tiding themselves over with a short-term job. His inner voice advised him to stay out of their way.

One evening like any other, he went to his caravan immediately after work, drank a beer sitting on the bed and gave himself a shot. Through the window, he saw two of the shady figures sitting on the yard fence, beer bottles in hand, talking. As they talked, one of them kept glancing and nodding in the direction of the caravan, so Munny could tell that they were discussing him. He locked up to be on the safe side.

He lay apathetically on his bed, staring at the yellowed, cracked ceiling. If in his delirium he focused on Maryam, he could actually see her and wanted to reach out to her. When he grasped at nothingness, bitter tears ran down his stubbled face. Then he saw her again. She had a serious face and looked at him earnestly.

He wanted to explain himself, but the vision disappeared and changed into another face. The eyes practically drilled into him. It was Voramay. She stared at him wordlessly. Her gaze pierced through him, her eyes reproachful and frightening. He trembled and rolled, moaning, on his side, like a small child, until sleep released him.

The next morning, he woke up with the same images in his head and shook himself. Normally, his nightmares didn't haunt him for so long or with such intensity.

He was late and dressed awkwardly. Damn! The farm owner was not to be messed with. He had eyes everywhere and would immediately notice a late arrival.

He was reprimanded for being late, and warned that he had better not do it again. As a disciplinary measure, he was given a longer shift that day because two of the workers had dropped out and there was a shortage of manpower.

He groaned to himself and snorted audibly. How could he keep going for so long without any drugs? During the short lunch break, when all the workers went to the farmhouse kitchen to get their food, he crept quietly to the caravan to take a small line of cocaine, so as to avoid attracting attention with withdrawal symptoms in the afternoon.

He hurried back to the farm and just managed to get a plate of beans and bacon. Unfocused and confused, he wondered if he had locked the caravan. Never mind, he had to look ahead now and get the job done as quickly as possible. He didn't want to attract any more attention.

When after work he sat down on the edge of his bed exhausted, intending to shoot up, the farm owner, accompanied by a few muscular labourers, burst open the door. 'You come with me!' he bellowed at him.

All those standing in front of the caravan stared in turn at Munny, the gear around him, and the rundown interior of the vehicle.

'Is this why you wanted me to give you the old scrap heap? You're a thief and a junkie.'

Munny was dragged roughly and painfully to the farmhouse by two strong men.

'And you two search everything,' the farmer shouted. 'The money must be there.'

Munny was shocked. Damon's stolen cash! Hopefully the hiding place was good enough. His pulse was racing, fear paralysed his thoughts.

In the farmhouse, the owner brusquely addressed him. 'Admit it, you took the cash from the sale of twenty sheep during your lunch break. A witness saw you sneaking away to the caravan. You must have hidden the money.'

Munny shook his head uncomprehendingly. He felt agitated. 'No, I didn't take anything. I wasn't in the house.' His body language, and his fear that Damon's money could be found, made him look untrustworthy and guilty in the eyes of the others.

'Liar! You can't be trusted. You're a junkie who always needs new drugs and money.' The farmer's face flushed red as he shouted. The veins on his neck bulged.

The two workers triumphantly returned with a small cloth bag, a nasty grin on their faces. 'Hey boss, we've got it. Look, here's the dosh.'

The owner glared at him. 'Get out of here, now! Consider yourself lucky I don't call the police!'

In desperation and anger, Munny shouted that this was a completely different sum of money and had nothing to do with the theft.

'I don't give a shit, the rest is probably from other thefts. Get out of here right now!'

His two bodyguards pushed him roughly towards the door. The other two grinned at each other as they stood in front of the farmhouse. 'Well, it seems we've come across a little money-spinner. Oh, and thank you for the loan.' The one pointed to the small cloth bag with Munny's supply of cocaine, which he had hidden in his shirt. 'That should bring a lot of dough on the market.' They laughed maliciously.

Munny wanted to jump them with his bare hands, but the strong arms carrying him away were remorseless.

'Just take your goddamn caravan and get the hell out of here,' the farmer shouted after him.

When they reached the vehicle, one of his guards punched him hard in the stomach. Munny collapsed and choked. While he was lying on the ground, the other kicked him hard in the back.

He got into the caravan and fled from the farm, groaning in agony. He left a high, red dust cloud behind him. He had lost everything. Tears of despair welled up in his eyes. He didn't know what distressed him more, the lack of money or the loss of the drugs. Everything went dark before his eyes. An urge to vomit overcame him and he had to stop at the side of the road.

He found a remote car park somewhere in the outback near Goolgowy. He lay apathetically in the caravan for days. All his strength seemed to have left him. The power of the drugs was burning him out.

Without cocaine, the chills increased and often caused him to collapse. The remaining petrol in the tank would not take him far. In his condition, all he could do was to lie apathetically in the caravan, close to fainting.

When he finally ran out of petrol, he decided to hitchhike to the northern outback. This was a real challenge. Few truck drivers dared to take such a down-and-out on the back of their truck. Sometimes a driver had the courage to let him ride up front, and offered him a sandwich out of pity.

One trucker recommended that he hitchhike to Cobar. There were cattle stations and mines there that would have jobs. Munny knew he needed a job to survive so he tried to get there. All the same, it was still a few hundred miles to Cobar and that could take days or even weeks. Right now was also the hottest time of year in the outback.

He made slow progress. His dishevelled appearance deterred many from giving him a lift and he had to walk long distances along the highway, sometimes in a trance, sometimes lost in an inner dialogue.

All he had left were a few hand-rolled joints. Too weak for what he needed, but better than nothing, he thought.

Shortly before the turnoff to Nymagee, his strength left him and he fell unconscious into the red dust of the roadside ditch.

He was dehydrated and had not eaten in days. As soon as he regained consciousness, he saw disturbing visions and hallucinations. His mother appeared to him and scolded him. Voramay stared at him like a snake. He roared at them both to stop it and give him Maryam back. Tears streamed down his cheeks, forming channels on his face which was smeared with red dust. The images were of such intensity that they tore his soul apart even more.

He rolled onto his back and looked up at the sun. 'Let go,' an inner voice told him.

Some vast emotion reared up in him. Was it despair, was it rage? He thought he heard the voice of Voramay again. 'In every

182

life lies the seed of death.' This time the voice sounded different, it sounded like the real Voramay.

He closed his eyes and thought to himself that the voice was actually right. His struggle was comfortless and full of torment. Why? He asked himself this question over and over again. In a kind of waking dream, he decided to follow that gentle voice and let go of his life. Powerless and burnt out as he was, it felt so tremendously light and liberating to lie here and breathe in the scent of the red soil. He was unspeakably tired. The merciless blazing sun stabbed him in the eyes when he opened them. Better to keep them closed. Disjointed thoughts raced through his mind, bellowing incessantly.

Few vehicles passed through the outback. Most were big trucks heading for the mines or transporting livestock for farms. He lay almost motionless for two days, as if paralysed, only partially waking every few hours to feel the heat of the day, before falling back into a comatose state.

Maryam threw herself passionately around his neck and embraced him. They fell onto a bed together. He felt her tender arms around him.

The dream burst.

Suddenly, other arms were reaching for him, like octopus tentacles. More and more arms embracing him tightly, threatening to throttle him. They dragged him away mercilessly. Screaming in fear, he reared up, thrashing around, trying to fend off all these hands.

As he looked with difficulty through the slits of his swollen eyes, the images of Maryam disappeared and he saw that several strong arms were heaving him onto the back of a small pick-up. He heard male and female voices, then he fell into a deep unconsciousness again, into a kind of weightlessness.

XIII. MISSION AUSTRALIA

Something warm flowed through his body. When he opened his eyes, he saw that he was in a simple room painted white. There was a tube in his arm. Was he dreaming again? Maryam would be coming soon. He closed his eyes and dozed off.

He heard a door open and blinked, looking up. A woman's face was leaning over him. He was taken aback, marvelling at how Maryam had changed.

The woman spoke to him. He looked at her. A woman in a white nurse's uniform. She smiled gently at him and tried to explain where he was. He was confused and looked around the room in panic. He didn't understand her and shook his head in confusion.

She carefully explained that he had almost died of dehydration. A driver from the Mission Australia mission station had discovered him in the ditch and brought him in. He was now in their infirmary.

Munny looked at her, bewildered. 'I'm alive? I can't believe it.' The nurse nodded. 'You still need to get your bearings. You've been having severe hallucinations. We had to tie you down and keep an eye on you to make sure you didn't hurt yourself. Just your withdrawal symptoms have been keeping us pretty busy here.' She raised an eyebrow and looked him straight in the face.

Munny turned his head to the side, shocked. His entire body ached. He grimaced. 'The pain will probably subside in a week,' she went on. 'It's the result of dehydration. Your muscles and fibres need fluids and nutrients. We've been giving them to you for the last seven days. That's how long you've been with us.'

'My God, as long as that?' He shook his head in disbelief and looked at the tube in his arm.

The nurse nodded and made a face, looking at the needle marks there. 'You went out into the dust and gave yourself a ruthless and radical detox. Not everyone survives something like that. Your body has suffered quite a bit. We've tried to give you nutrient solutions. It was all we could do.' She shrugged her shoulders with resignation and put a large bottle of water in front of him. Strangely enough, he had no desire to drink. Probably because they'd been filling him with the nutrient solution for days, he thought ruefully. He wouldn't have objected to a bottle or two of beer right now, but that option probably wasn't available at the moment.

He looked at the nurse, listless and with empty eyes. She shook her head, finding him taciturn, probably thinking him ungrateful, and left the room.

During the next few days, while he lay idly in bed, many thoughts went through his mind. Gradually he found himself no longer missing the boost of the daily drug intake as much as at the beginning. His mind was slowly learning to concentrate and remember for longer periods again. However, the more his head cleared, the more he realised he was still missing many parts of the last few weeks and months. Inwardly, he cursed himself repeatedly for the situation he had got himself into.

He felt at a loss as to what he should do next. Back to the hotel in Sydney? He couldn't remember Dang's phone number. His mind went into an endless loop in which he kept trying to re-member – only to realise, resigned and angry with himself, that his memory was still letting him down.

The calm thoughtful nurse was a good influence on him. He

gradually became more open and learned more about the state in which he had been found. Slowly his memory gaps filled in and revealed a picture. His sense of time also improved increasingly. Maryam and Estelle had died over a year ago.

After a few more days, he decided that once he was able to stand up again he had to get out of the sterile hospital ward as soon as possible. He asked the doctor and nurses what options were available to him after he was discharged. The doctor on duty that day promised to put him in touch with the head of the mission. 'Just stop by our Thérèse's office and discuss it with her; she always has some use for new arrivals. The mission never runs out of jobs, only helping hands.' He winked encouragingly at Munny.

He felt so useless! Ashamed of his situation, he resigned himself to taking on simple duties in the mission from now on.

The following week, he reported to Thérèse's office. She was originally from Brittany and had been in charge of all matters in the house for about twenty years. She explained to him briefly, concisely and very firmly the aims of the mission, and what kind of people it catered for. She left him in no doubt about the high level of discipline that prevailed.

Attached to Mission Australia was a school for orphaned or impoverished children aged six to twenty-one.

'Our first priority is to ensure that the children are well looked after. I can offer you a kind of caretaker job. You would be solely responsible for the school section. You will ensure that the rooms are kept spotlessly clean. You will also be responsible for repairs. If replacements are needed, please let me know. If necessary, you will create a list. You will also work for a wage that we will determine. Half the cost of your treatment, which the mission has already paid for you, will be deducted from that wage in monthly instalments. The mission will cover the rest. Do you understand that, and are you ready for the work that lies ahead of you?' She left no doubt about the seriousness of her words. Munny felt transported back to his schooldays, when he had been unequivocally made to understand, in just the same way, what tasks awaited him.

'Once your debt is paid off,' she continued without waiting for his reaction, 'we will have another talk, if that is what you still want.' She looked at him questioningly over the rim of her glasses. 'I will then make you a new offer. Of course, that also depends on how you turn out.' She raised her eyebrows. 'We'll see in six months' time.'

Munny nodded, inwardly alarmed, his head bowed. He had never felt so small and insignificant in his life. Thérèse looked at him with her ice-blue eyes and held out a sheet of paper. 'Here, please sign this. The second sheet is your timetable. If anything out of the ordinary comes up, I'll let you know.' She cleared her throat awkwardly. 'I don't need to tell you that drugs and alcohol are forbidden here. So take this as a second chance, and stay away from them!'

Despite her uncompromising words, she smiled gently at him for the first time. Her expression calmed him and made up a bit for her curt manner.

His day began at six in the morning. He would sweep the four classrooms and the teachers' room, and clear away rubbish. Only when the lessons began did he go to the children's dormitories and mop the floor. At the same time, he kept an inventory of anything that was missing or needed repairing. At ten o'clock, the auxiliary staff at the mission were given a short ten-minute break with coffee and sweet pastries. He loved this break because he finally got something to eat and drink. It reminded him of old days at the hotel.

He got to know the staff, his colleagues at the mission. Most of them, like him, had ended up here because life had given them a raw deal.

He was particularly struck by a highly introverted young Eurasian man with a skinny build. Everyone called him Sunny. He plainly had a New Zealand father and a Thai mother. His real name was Sunan, but everyone had christened him Sunny from the start because of his politeness and his ready laugh.

Munny found himself sitting with him more and more during breaks. Sunny explained to him in great detail how the mission worked and who was responsible for what. The more opportunity they had to talk, the more Munny learned about his story.

Sunny's parents had separated when he was thirteen. His mother went back to Thailand alone without warning and left him behind. His father, who had a full-time job as a construction worker, never had time for him. Sunny joined street gangs. He was eventually caught breaking and entering with his gang at the age of fifteen, and put into a home.

Here things went from bad to worse. The older boys in the home were organised into gangs, and he was subjected to bullying. 'You know, it was basically a big bunch of criminal youths and the inexperienced remainder who were criminalised by the others, like me,' Sunny added, staring at the table.

When he was increasingly mistreated, coerced and harassed by the other inmates, he took the opportunity to escape from the poorly supervised establishment. While hitchhiking, he heard about Mission Australia from the drivers who picked him up, and decided to stay here. That was almost ten years ago.

Sunny reminded him a little of Dang, except that Sunny was tall and lanky and had a gentle, quiet manner and delicate hands like a watchmaker's. As Munny listened to his account, he had to shake his head again and again, thinking of Dang's life story and his own fate as a foundling.

Sunny too looked sympathetic when Munny, not sparing any of the details, described the course of his life, which in the end had not been any the less of a rough ride.

They met in the evening after work in the mission canteen, which stayed open for staff to eat late.

Sunny made a face at the sight of the evening meal tray. 'I'm surprised that you, as a former star chef, can put up with it. The ingredients are very basic and mostly overcooked. Even the children don't like it, but their hunger gets the better of them.' He smiled wryly.

Munny nodded. 'Yes, when you look at the children, they don't seem particularly well-fed. But that's probably more of a cost issue. I think Thérèse keeps a pretty tight hold on the purse strings.'

'That could well be, because the mission is partly state-sponsored and partly has to depend on its own income. I guess that can't be much,' said Sunny.

Munny scratched his head thoughtfully.

After three months, he had found a certain normality and a new rhythm of life. In a peculiar way, this gave him inner stability. He had his addiction under control, though it cost him a brutal effort. Even the urge for hard liquor was almost completely gone. A cold lager now and then would have been nice after a hard day's work, but since no one here consumed alcohol, it wasn't particularly difficult for him to do without.

A young doctor from the infirmary came to join their evening meetings. Her name was Mel, and she was in her first year on the job after graduating. She had a boyish and uncomplicated manner, probably stemming from her job. Her reddish shoulder-length hair was in fascinating contrast to her green eyes and the freckles on her nose. At twenty-eight years of age, she radiated a pure zest for life and laughed a lot.

'Where are you from originally?' Munny wanted to know.

'About five years ago, my parents got tired of living in London and settled in Melbourne. My father works in the office of an international freight company, and my mother is a receptionist at one of the larger law firms in the city. I started my medical studies in England, and completed them here.'

Munny felt she was a determined character. A woman who took things into her own hands. Munny liked her casual, relaxed manner and there was a fascinating aura about her and her green eyes that captivated him.

'Well, I guess you've already heard my not very creditable story.' Munny pursed his lips and scratched the back of his head. She nodded seriously and looked him in the eye.

He told her how the mission had pulled him out of the ditch and saved him from the depths of drug and alcohol addiction. He was grateful for this turning point in his life.

'Man, you can count yourself lucky that your body was able to withstand all that and your heart didn't give out altogether,' Mel said warmly. 'That was a radical detox for you.' She raised an eyebrow. 'Many suffer cardiac arrests or are partially paralysed after a stroke. Well, weeds flourish when flowers perish, I guess.' She laughed out loud at this, and poked him in the ribs.

Sunny grinned to himself and winked in agreement.

Munny became more and more engaged in the warm, open relationship with his colleagues and was happy to make new contacts. It was a bit like old times with Maryam and Dang, he thought wistfully. Slowly he was recovering from the sense that he had been torn out of his life, as he came to accept his new life increasingly from day to day. He was able to reflect more deeply on Voramay's teachings, which gave him something to hold on to.

Gradually, his enthusiasm for work returned to its old level.

The children loved his jokes and hung on his every word in the evenings before going to bed, listening to his stories about his homeland. They had endless questions – even the older ones, who had never seen anything but the red earth of the outback. They couldn't believe how fertile and green it must be in Cambodia. Munny waxed enthusiastic about the rice paddies and about Khmer cuisine with its different vegetables and fruits, which he himself set such store by.

A shy little girl named Lara whispered in a tiny voice that she would love to have a meal as good as the one Munny had described. The others nodded in agreement.

'We always get the same here. There are hardly any vegetables. Just apples from town now and then when new deliveries arrive,' said a tall narrow-chested fourteen-year-old boy. 'Could you maybe put in a good word for us in the kitchen?'

'Oh yes, please,' someone said.

Everyone nodded. 'They'll listen to you.'

The group of children looked at him expectantly with wide open eyes. Munny was touched by so much trust and high hopes. 'I'll see what I can do with Thérèse,' he murmured to himself.

The children beamed at him gratefully.

'I can't promise anything, do you hear me? And don't pull long faces if it doesn't work out.'

Munny lay in bed late that night, arms folded behind his head, unable to sleep. The children's pitiful requests haunted him. He reflected that there were only two months left to run on his agreement with Thérèse. He could perhaps ask her for a new role and at the same time raise the issue of the canteen and kitchen. His knowledge of the calculations for food purchases could be useful here. He also decided to talk to her about his future career here at the mission. She was usually a little more willing to consider new things on Mondays.

He took Sunny into his confidence and told him what he had planned.

'Cool, that's a great idea, we would all benefit from it. Just show her what's possible with the means available.'

Munny was still uncertain whether his initiative might not be seen as presumptuous. Did a former addict even deserve a leap of faith? Anyway, he had nothing to lose. Either Thérèse had a job for him or she didn't.

'Come in.'

Munny entered the room somewhat hesitantly. He fumbled uncertainly with his caretaker's uniform. The head of the mission, who was perhaps sixty years old, was sitting behind her desk at six o'clock, as she did every morning. She looked up from what she was reading and regarded him with astonishment. She pushed her glasses to the tip of her nose, and curiously gazed at Munny over the top of them with her ice-blue eyes.

'Good morning,' Munny said awkwardly. She nodded briefly, still keeping her eyes on him.

Munny bowed respectfully. 'Could I ask you a quick question?'

'Yes, of course. Do you have a problem?'

Munny shifted nervously from one foot to the other.

She pointed to a chair in front of her desk. 'Sit down.'

'Well, I wanted to ... well ... ask if you're planning on continuing to employ me at the mission ... since our initial agreement expires in six weeks.'

Thérèse took the glasses off her nose and laid them on the table as she leaned back. 'Well, I've heard you're doing a good job. You seem to have found your way back to an exceptionally disciplined life. That's commendable. You also seem to be well liked by the children and by your colleagues. I would like you to stay with us. You're very organised as a caretaker, I like that, and we would be happy if you could continue your work here.'

Munny fidgeted and stared at the floor.

'Or do you have something else in mind? Do you want to leave?'

Munny opened his eyes wide in shock. 'No, I like it here ... I ... um ... actually wanted to ask if ... well, I have an idea. Maybe it could actually work. You know, when I was a star chef, before I went to pieces, I was responsible for food purchasing and costing. I thought to myself, maybe if you need someone to take over the purchasing, I could do that. And perhaps you need a cook. Actually, I think you need one urgently, given the ... quality of the food that comes out of the kitchen.' He bit his tongue. Hopefully he hadn't overstepped the mark with his choice of words.

After a long pause, during which Thérèse looked as if she were studying the surface of her desk for any notches, she looked up and smiled. 'Well, that was pretty direct. Don't forget, I eat the same as everyone else here. But you're right, we do need better quality. And you think you can get that at same cost as before?'

Munny nodded cautiously. 'Why don't you just let me handle the budget and I'll see what I can do.' He had regained his composure and sensed that Thérèse was not entirely averse to his idea. 'We could grow all the vegetables and other stuff we need in the back garden. I would take care of it. The children could be involved too. You could even give them training, perhaps.'

Thérèse looked at him in amazement. 'Well, it seems you have it all worked out. Make a list for me of what we need. You can also study our food shopping list. We can't afford to spend any more than that.' She rummaged in a folder and pulled out a sheet of paper. 'Here, this is from last month. If you can make your idea work and we all get better quality food, I'm fine with it.' She screwed up her face into a real laugh for the first time. 'Welcome to the club, Munny, you're in!'

Munny laughed cheekily at her. 'Yes, sir!'

'And don't forget who you're dealing with, okay?

Munny grinned mischievously. 'No need to tell me that.'

She raised her eyebrows and shot him a glance of mock severity.

As Munny left the office, inwardly jubilant, he glanced at his watch. Today his shift in the dormitories didn't start till seven. So there was still time to catch Mel in the infirmary. He found her in the hall outside the sickrooms, holding a medical file in her hands.

'Mel, you won't believe the news.' He rushed up to her. She looked at him intently with her green eyes as he told her, then spontaneously threw her arms around his neck and kissed him on the cheek. 'Finally something decent to eat! Munny, that is sensational. Have you told Sunny? I think he suffers even more than the children from the daily slop he gets given.'

'I'll tell him later. I won't see him now until he finishes to-night.' Only now did Munny realise that Mel was still holding both his hands in her euphoria. He couldn't help embracing her with enthusiasm. She wrapped her arms around him. It felt so good and familiar somehow, he thought to himself. They held each other close.

'Munny, I'm so happy for you. And for all of us, of course. After all, there's nothing like good nutrition. Trust me, I'm a doctor.' She grinned at him, her cheeks rosy, and gave him a playful shove.

Sunny was delighted and amazed. 'You simply must cook Khmer cuisine. I'm sure it will agree with me a whole lot better.' He patted his stomach and beamed with contentment.

Late that evening, Munny studied the shopping lists. 'I can do better than that,' he thought to himself and made a few notes. His ideas were bubbling over. He developed a completely new scheme that went way beyond the previous practices and possibilities of the canteen. He was curious to see what Thérèse would say. Would she find his ideas too bold? She was a very rational woman. But as long as the cost factor was right, and no one else had to spend any extra time realising his plan, it should all work.

He fell asleep with his notes on his stomach, exhausted. When he opened his eyes in the morning, it was as if he had been transported to a new era. His unbeatable instinct and strength of will were with him again, as if out of nowhere. He felt as if he had been transplanted back to his time at Raffles, when Luc had trusted him with all the kitchen plans. I'm back again, he thought, smiling to himself.

Before he shared his ideas with Thérèse, he wanted to get Mel's opinion. Her clear-eyed way of seeing things was a touchstone for him. He arranged to meet her at lunchtime.

Mel nodded in approval. 'Wow, that would make our canteen a real restaurant. An open kitchen and a buffet. I'm all for it, there'll be more choice all round, and everything will look much more appetising. Here's an idea. Before you talk to Thérèse, why don't you surprise her with your style of cuisine. Give yourself a morning off and just take over the kitchen – preferably on a day when a new delivery arrives. That way you would have more options for putting your ideas into practice. The kitchen team will definitely go along with it, and they can all learn something new.'

Munny thought Mel's idea was brilliant. Spontaneously, he took her hands and looked deep into her eyes. 'You know, Mel, you're the person in my life who means the most to me. I ... I ... er, I've fallen in love with you. I hope this isn't too much for you to take. I don't know how to put it any other way.' He scratched his neck awkwardly, looking up at her questioningly, his head bowed.

She returned the look silently, smiling broadly. Her eyes sparkled mysteriously. Then she took his face in both hands and kissed him on the lips. 'Munny, I feel the same way. Ever since I met you. I just didn't dare say anything.'

'Really?'

She nodded, her cheeks flushed. Munny pulled her to him across the table and kissed her passionately. At last he could feel the voice of his heart again. He ran his fingers through her shoulder-length hair and pressed his head firmly against her forehead. Mel wrapped her arms around his neck. They were alone now in the small visitors' room at the infirmary.

'I'd like to see you every day and spend as much time with you as possible ... what do you think?'

She nodded, her eyes lowered.

He raised her head and kissed her passionately once more. He was happy again for the first time since Maryam's death. He felt as if he were walking on air.

Munny prepared well for his secret cooking debut. He studied the food order lists for days and thought about what he could make from them. Despite the small budget, there were excellent possibilities. He decided to prepare fresh stir-fried vegetables with a curry. Before that, a Thai chicken soup. Everything had to be fresh and quickly prepared in view of the large number of portions. It was also a training session for him, considering that his last assignment had been over a year ago. The kitchen staff were open-minded and did a reasonable job of preparing the ingredients according to his instructions.

The previous chef was not overly enthusiastic about the change to his monotonous daily schedule. For him, it meant a major adjustment. Munny sensed that a failure of his project would be what the man was secretly hoping for. He probably could not expect much support from this quarter.

Intensely focused, he watched every move in the kitchen like a hawk. Above all, he didn't want to look foolish in front of Mel. Just the thought of her made him smile. Her fresh, carefree and boyish manner did him good and motivated him. Sunny rubbed his hands at the prospect of a change of menu. 'Finally someone is taking charge. It's about time!'

On his day off, he disappeared into the kitchen early in the morning to check everything before the others arrived. His inner restlessness reminded him vividly of the competition in Singapore. He sensed that today could be a turning point. Inwardly tense, he clenched his hands into fists.

Five minutes till the break. Although everything had been perfectly prepared, he checked it all for the third time. The others around him in the kitchen grinned and smirked. 'Come on, Munny, this isn't a five-star restaurant. Calm down. They'll survive your food and get over the culture shock.'

Everyone laughed. Munny just glared at them, shaking his head. One of them nudged him. 'Come on, man, stay cool. You'll see, it'll go like clockwork.'

The slightly spicy lemongrass soup with chicken, rice and lots of Thai basil had been served up. He peered through a narrow gap in the door of the kitchen. From the looks of it, there was some murmuring going on at the staff tables. Mel and Sunny, being in the know, ate in silence, with a hidden grin on their faces.

When the main course was served and people started to eat, an unmistakable murmur ran through the room. Munny tried to spot Thérèse at one of the tables. She was eating impassively. He realised with disappointment that she didn't seem to notice any change and was oblivious of her surroundings. Strange. He couldn't fathom her behaviour. After dessert, he helped clear up in the kitchen, and then slipped back to his room to get changed for his afternoon job.

Clueless as to how to interpret all this, he looked glum. He had given it his all! But the verdict of the staff at the mission was overwhelming. Word had got around that he was behind the whole operation. Mel threw her arms around his neck and kissed him in front of everyone. She didn't care what the others might think.

'Munny, that was the best meal we've had for ages! Simply sensational!'

Sunny rose to his feet and began clapping, his grin growing wider. More and more clapping hands joined in until the whole room was standing and applauding. Munny shook his head in disbelief and took an emotional bow before the assembled crowd.

The next morning, he knocked on the door of Thérèse's office with a stack of sorted papers, summarising his new approach. His neck artery was throbbing. Would he be able to convey his plans in a clear and comprehensible way?

Thérèse looked up at him with her usual poker face. 'Sit down.' After a pause, she took off her glasses and gazed at him across the table.

'So, I see. You used your day off yesterday to convince us of your culinary skills. Hmmmm ...' She paused thoughtfully and looked at him hard. 'Well, I must say you succeeded. Triumphed, even! But you know ... this isn't a Michelin-starred restaurant. We have to keep the costs under control. What you cook costs money. You know we have to watch the finances around here!'

Munny was prepared for this objection. Without saying a word, he handed her the budget for yesterday's meal compared with the costs of the previous regime. The old system had actually been even more expensive.

Thérèse frowned in astonishment. 'Not bad, not bad.'

Munny grinned and handed her his sketches and designs for the more attractive restaurant he had in mind, with takeaway options for external visitors. The idea had occurred to him because highway truckers were always walking in and asking if they offered food. Word would spread quickly, and the income would be a great help to the mission. More guests could be accommodated than in the old impersonal dining hall. A few minor structural changes would have to be made, opening up the whole area from the kitchen to the restaurant, and a sign would have to be put up on the outside of the building.

When he suggested setting up a culinary school like the one Paul had had in Siem Reap, Thérèse gave a thoughtful nod.

Munny cleared his throat carefully. 'After finishing school, the older ones could get to know the full range of the restaurant sector. Given training, they could find jobs in hotels or restaurants. I've put together a cost breakdown and a detailed timeline here.' He pulled the paper out of the documents in front of her. 'The renovation could be done during the school holidays, so no one would be disturbed.' He presented everything to Thérèse with great care, answering her questions and addressing all her objections and concerns. He tried to detect signs of approval in her eyes. But she remained extremely businesslike. She would certainly have been a good poker player.

Finally, she smiled openly at him. 'Munny, I have to give you a lot of credit. For your plans, of course, but also for yourself. When they brought you to us and I learned what had happened to you, I honestly didn't think there was the slightest chance that you'd get back on track. I congratulate you on that, and on your discipline! And, of course, in a way, we deserve some credit as well.' She grinned at him confidently. 'You're a real asset. We don't want to be without you here in the house anymore, and from what I've heard, the children seem to have taken a liking to you as well. I'll think about your plans and let you know next week.' With a broad, reassuring smile on her face, she dismissed him from her office.

XIV. FULL CIRCLE

He almost flew to the infirmary to find Mel. 'I'd like to invite you to town this weekend. There might be something to celebrate.' He grinned at her. 'But if you don't want to, I can look for other company.'

Mel pinched his side and laughed. 'You watch it!' She kissed him. 'Of course we'll go.'

Munny went to the gym that evening to train. He had started to rebuild his muscles some months ago and now he felt particularly motivated. His appearance had largely reverted to what it had been, thanks to his regular lifestyle here at the mission. His face, which had become gaunt as a result of his drug excesses, was fuller again.

Around his eyes and mouth, the past had left its mark in the form of pronounced wrinkles. His chin looked more angular due to the slightly narrower shape of his face, and his high cheekbones were more prominent. For his thirty-eight years, he looked mature and charismatic. His expressive eyes and calm manner gave him a mysterious air.

He and Mel had been lovers for a month or so. Munny felt magically drawn to Mel. He would never have dreamed that he would be able to feel so much love and tenderness for a woman again. Mel gave him the space he needed. She was a highly empathetic and intelligent woman who touched him less with words than with her sporty, boyish spontaneity. The harmony and balance that radiated from her did him a world of good.

Munny had now been given his own small apartment by the mission, where he could retreat after work. Mel stayed with him more and more often overnight. It gave him great pleasure on her free evenings to take her naked body in his arms and caress her skin tenderly.

He loved the way she wrapped herself around him, showing her desire for him. He let her have her way with him, and then made love to her again and again with unbridled desire. Her soft, throaty moans when he penetrated her and she pushed against him excited him and inspired him to do more.

Drained after their intense lovemaking, he stroked her hair, caressed her cheeks and felt her firm breasts responding to his hands. Their bodies pressed passionately against each other until they fell asleep from exhaustion.

Munny enjoyed waking up next to her in the morning and gazing at her relaxed, sleeping face at close range. He gently brushed his lips over her slightly open mouth and kissed her carefully so as not to wake her. Half asleep, she pressed her forehead against his cheek. He smiled at this unconscious gesture of affection and drew the blanket up over her half-uncovered naked body.

'What are you doing?' Mel whispered as she woke up, blinking.

'I'm watching you in your sleep,' he whispered tenderly. 'You look so innocent, I love the sight of you so much.'

'Hm, that's very private,' she smiled.

'I know, that's why these moments belong only to me.' He kissed her tenderly and held her close.

He felt the excitement rising inside him. Mel was rubbing against him, visibly aroused. He pushed her legs apart.

Mel moaned, 'I want you so badly.'

An ear-splitting siren suddenly made them start up. At first, Munny didn't know what to make of it.

'Munny, I think that's the fire alarm.'

They hastily gathered up their clothes, got dressed, and ran downstairs.

It was pandemonium down there. An employee ran past them, struggling to carry two fire extinguishers. 'Munny, here, grab this one and come with me. There's a fire in the kitchen.' He thrust it into his hand.

When they arrived, all they saw was black smoke billowing from the swinging door. Some people who had been trying to extinguish the fire emerged, coughing. Firefighters wearing breathing masks were among them. Sunny came running out, coughing and out of breath.

'My God, Sunny, what's going on here?' Munny shouted at him.

'No idea, a cook just told me that someone was preparing a wok on the gas stove for lunch. Seems he waited too long before adding oil to the overheated pan. Drops fell and triggered a flash fire. His colleagues rushed to help, and the panicky dimwits tried to put it out with water.' Sunny tapped his finger on his forehead.

'This can't be happening,' Munny groaned. 'Now of all times.'

Mel asked if there were any injuries. At that moment her beeper went off. 'I have to go.' She ran to the infirmary.

Munny grabbed hold of a firefighter. 'How bad is the damage?"

The man took off his mask, exhausted. His face was covered with beads of sweat. 'Hard to say, but I think a large part of the kitchen is gone.' He put the mask back on. Not waiting for further questions, he hurried back to the heavily blackened and devastated kitchen to help with the clean-up. The flames were voracious. They engulfed the entire kitchen area.

Thérèse stood behind them, her hand over her mouth in shock. She had overheard the conversation with the firefighter.

'Come on, Thérèse,' Munny said, 'luckily it's only property damage. The three men in the infirmary are being checked out. You'll see, they'll be fine in no time.'

She turned and hurried to the infirmary.

Munny tugged at his hair. What bad luck for him, now that he had finally been able to take over kitchen operations. It would take months to get everything back to normal. Damn it to hell! He also felt sorry for Mel, who had been preparing to qualify as a doctor here. It wouldn't be the same relaxed, calm environment she needed anymore.

He would have to talk to Thérèse later. She always had a practical solution.

He joined a colleague for the improvised dinner that followed. They cooked whatever they could quickly put together without a professional kitchen. Fortunately, the supplies had been well sealed off behind the kitchen in a large storage room. Munny used all his imagination to get something creative on the plate despite the limitations of what was available.

'Munny, could you please drop in on Thérèse tomorrow morning? I was with her just now, and she asked me to tell you.' His colleague gave him an appreciative pat on the back.

Privately, Munny hoped that Thérèse had something up her sleeve. He wanted to resume his plans as soon as possible.

The next morning, Thérèse was standing behind her desk and, to Munny's amazement, his sketches were spread out in front of her. She was leaning over the papers when he entered. Visibly pleased to see him, she beckoned him to her and motioned for him to stand beside her at the desk.

She placed her hand on his arm. 'Tell me, what did you have in mind here?' She pointed to the diagram of an outdoor area connected to the main building by a walkway.

'Well, I thought of a small outdoor dining area, directly connected to the kitchen school inside. When travelling diners arrive, they could sit under the trees in the garden. The service staff wouldn't have to walk long distances between the school kitchen and outside. This area would be self-sufficient. The main kitchen stays where it is and just needs to be opened on one side.' Munny took a deep breath. 'I think the fire damage makes it all the more necessary. Or do you just want to plaster the cracks and paint it? Besides, these walls are ancient and dilapidated. It was due for renovation anyway.' He looked at her expectantly.

'Don't talk about our old premises like that, they've served us well since long before your time. But the fire has given the whole thing a new urgency ... I'm considering taking a leap forward and doing more than just repairs. Your idea of a restaurant, a takeaway and a cooking school is a risk, you know?' Thérèse furrowed her brow in thought.

Munny nodded. He recalled what Voramay had said in situations where he had doubted himself and his plans.

'Thérèse, I don't want to tread on your toes, but my old friend and mentor always told me: "Only those who set out will discover new land, and setting out for new shores is also the search for new horizons." So, why don't we go for it and take a chance?'

Thérèse sucked in an audible breath and scratched her chin. She looked alternately out of the window and at Munny.

After what felt like an eternity, she put her hand on his shoulder. 'All right, we'll do it. You're responsible for costs and coordination with the workmen, especially in terms of time. Get offers, calculate everything, and we'll discuss it. In particular, work out the budget minus what the insurance pays and what the mission can contribute from its own funds. This investment has to be covered by your estimated income, or we won't get it past the board of trustees.' She looked at him earnestly over the rim of her glasses. 'We also have to be careful not to disrupt regular operations with construction work. It has to be done during the coming summer holidays. Do you understand how much is at stake here?'

Of course Munny was aware of all this. He nodded and looked at her with grateful eyes. 'Thank you, Thérèse. I won't let you down.'

For the first time, Thérèse took his hand in hers and held it, nodding and saying nothing. 'Thank you, Munny, for your dedication. Get in touch as soon as you have results. Time is short.'

The renovation was surprisingly fast and efficient. Thérèse had been able to speed up the process a bit through a board member who had connections with the insurance company. This way the mission did not have to provide interim finance for the project which saved a lot of time and money.

As Munny had planned, the big wall of the old kitchen was removed and the dining room opened up, while at the same time a passage to the training kitchen and refreshments stand was created in a part of the quiet, shady garden.

He personally supervised the renovation work and coordinated it so that they would not run into time constraints. The inauguration ceremony was planned for just after the school holidays. He was extremely proud to be able to meet the deadline as planned. Thérèse was looking forward to the reopening in a fever of expectation. This wasn't at all like the cool-headed mission head Munny knew. He enjoyed watching the eagerness with which she planned the opening ceremony, together with the board and all the mission staff. Two weeks after school started, the garden and the new building interior were decorated in the mission's colours, white and pink, and ready for the inauguration. Small strings of lights were to illuminate the newly laid out garden at nightfall.

Munny looked proudly at Thérèse. 'Isn't this a romantic setting?'

'Yes, very much so! You'll see me here more often after work, too. I'm afraid I'll be around for much of the evening – you won't be getting rid of me anytime soon.' She looked at him with mock seriousness.

Munny laughed heartily. 'Oh dear, not that too!'

'Have I already told you that I got the training licence for your cooking school?' She winked at him. 'A member of the board smoothed the way considerably for us and was able to speed up the formalities. So we'll be ready to start at the beginning of next year.' She rubbed her hands together.

Munny was extremely proud of what they had all achieved.

Mel was able to prepare for the final exam of her medical training despite the noise from the construction site. After weeks of intensive study, she was successfully registered with the Medical Board of Australia and was beside herself with joy and of course pride when she showed him the licence.

'Munny, I can hardly believe it. I can now practise medicine independently and choose where to set up my own practice. You have no idea what a huge weight has been lifted from my mind!' She laughed and impetuously threw her arms around his neck.

Now more than ever, Munny wanted to show Mel that he could follow through on his plans. He prepared meticulously for a speech at the inauguration ceremony – his first! Nothing could be allowed to go wrong. His old ambition had resurfaced.

Munny surprised everyone at the inauguration ceremony with a speech in which he first praised Thérèse and then Mel, not without mentioning her success in becoming a doctor.

'As you all probably know, Mel and I found each other here. She is an amazing and reflective woman – my dream woman. That I am standing before you today having recovered my form ...' He broke off, grinning and laughing at some sly comments coming from the guests about his 'form'. ' … As I said, I have my Mel to thank for my form. She got me back into shape and good health again.'

Massive applause broke out. Munny looked first at Mel and then at Thérèse in the midst of the guests, laughing and slightly embarrassed.

He cleared his throat. 'By the way, Mel told me today that she has decided to accept Thérèse's offer on behalf of the mission, and take up her first job here as a doctor.'

Everyone applauded enthusiastically at Munny's speech and laughed at his little jokes about Thérèse's strict management style. Thérèse looked at him with a face of mock indignation, which made everyone laugh.

Mel kissed him on the cheek and beamed at him in front of everyone.

He sensed a change taking place within him. For the first time, he felt he had arrived. A warm feeling of harmony spread through him, and seemed to rub off on those around him.

'A toast to the mission, and to the happy couple!' One of the board members next to Thérèse raised his glass.

Samsara, as Voramay always said. Eventually the circle closes.

XV. HEAVEN ON EARTH

Word spread quickly about the garden restaurant and the takeaway with its Asian-influenced Khmer cuisine, especially since the garden was a cosy place to sit under the tall trees at the height of summer and in the transitional seasons.

If demand continued at this rate, more outdoor seating would be needed. Surprisingly, Munny's idea of opening the garden to outside guests for dinner as well on certain weekend evenings was met with enthusiasm by Thérèse. This would encourage many visitors from the city to leave their sweltering streets for a few hours' getaway during the summer.

The children from the middle school years were already learning to take on simple tasks in the service area and kitchen outside their lessons. The success of 'their' little restaurant motivated them no end.

Munny was pleased to have adopted Paul's idea from Siem Reap in its entirety. Even vegetables, salads and spices were grown in specially created beds behind the mission, to be harvested and used in the kitchen. The children enjoyed the cooking school immensely, especially as it provided a welcome change from their normal school routine.

It moved him deeply to see how the children developed individual initiative. Some of them came to him with their ideas. He gave them every freedom and allowed them to be creative in implementing their plans, even when he knew that in terms of taste it was not always the best solution.

But he remembered his own beginnings, when he sometimes aimed too high and only realised afterwards that he had set himself too great a challenge. Well, if you don't dream of flying, you won't grow wings. This wisdom had proven true in his life. But who knows, he smiled to himself as he acknowledged their ambition, maybe they will grow wings next time.

On opening night, after all the guests had left, Munny sat on a large swing they had set up for the children on the sturdy branches of a tall old tree. Mel was on his lap, his arms wrapped around her. 'Sweetheart,' he said, 'let's stay together forever. It's just so good to be with you.' He inhaled the perfume on her neck. Mel turned sideways to whisper in his ear. 'Hmmm,' she murmured mysteriously, 'but you have to promise me something ...'

Munny looked at her questioningly. 'Anything you want.'

She smiled. 'If I had known that earlier ... No, I'm only joking, but if it's to be forever, you must promise me you'll live to be at least ninety, I won't settle for anything less,' she whispered into his ear, smiling.

He laughed with relief. 'I promise.'

'Okay,' she breathed. 'Then I'll stay forever.'

He kissed her on the neck and held her tight.

'I love having your strong arms around me, I feel so safe,' she said.

'That's because you are,' he whispered.

In the course of the next six months, word of the success of the cooking class spread like wildfire. They were now fully booked a good two weeks in advance. In view of the profits that could be made, Thérèse decided to expand the small restaurant in mid-season, with a view to the end of the year. She herself was a regular guest at the weekends with her friends and acquaintances.

The extension was completed quickly and was finished by the beginning of the following year. The cooking school building was also expanded somewhat, as the group of trainees had grown rapidly. This was not least because Munny's gentle and sensitive way of passing on his knowledge to 'his' children was much appreciated and produced great results. The children really idolised him. More often than not, the little ones came to him before going to bed wanting to hear another story about Voramay and the temples of Siem Reap. He loved to recreate the magic around his old friend again and again. At last he felt her speaking to him once more, as if she were gazing at him with her wise and loving eyes.

Even the national press attended the opening of the expanded culinary school, along with city officials. Word quickly spread about the project, and it was taken as a model for several other Mission Australia branches. The front-page story, with a picture of Thérèse and her team, was fantastic and made perfect advertising. To his amazement, Munny got a column to himself and a picture. He was also interviewed. The idea of offering training in the restaurant while putting the profits into the school's further development was a clear winner. No one thought the ten percent surcharge on menu prices, which was reinvested as a contribution to the training programme, was money ill spent.

Munny was absorbed in his new role. He felt comfortable and accepted in his new family – even if they weren't his own children. All this made up for what had been taken from him.

What would Estelle look like now? He suppressed the thought, as he still carried the endless grief and pain for the loss of his two dearest people within him. Voramay would have told him to look at what was around him, pointing to the fact that he now had a much larger family.

My goodness, he thought to himself, how many deeply painful

and devastating losses do you have to get through in life? He shook his head. It was a depressing thought.

'Munny, someone's asking for you outside.' A voice tore him out of his thoughts. Leo, one of the older apprentices, came puffing into the kitchen from the garden, red-cheeked and laden with bowls.

'Well, he'll have to wait until I've blanched the vegetables with the shrimps. It's probably just another journalist.'

Leo nodded and ran back out into the evening-lit garden with the starters.

After making a few preparations, Munny remembered that Leo had mentioned a visitor.

He went to the table indicated, at the edge of the garden. There, in the semi-darkness, sat a man alone at the table. He might have been about Munny's age. With his close-cropped hair and alert eyes, he followed the scene attentively from his corner table.

The man saw Munny approaching. He jumped up spontaneously and came towards him, smiling in a friendly way and studying his face.

Munny's eyes widened. This couldn't be happening!

'Man, buddy, I finally tracked you down! I can't tell you how happy that article in the paper made me. You're alive! My goodness, how often have I asked myself what had become of you in the past year and a half.'

It was Dang!

Tears welled up in Munny's eyes. He had often wondered how Dang might be doing, but he'd never dared to contact the hotel in Sydney to ask about him. He was still too ashamed of his inglorious departure. He wouldn't even have been able to give his name over the phone. After all the bad publicity he had caused, most of the hotel staff would still remember his name very well, and not in a pleasant way.

Much moved, Dang fell on Munny's neck, and they shook each other's shoulders repeatedly, both of them incredulous. Dang stood before him with tears in his eyes, shaking his head in disbelief.

'Do you have time?'

Munny nodded wordlessly and indicated the table. They sat down. Dang looked him deep in the eyes. 'I don't believe it! It's the old Munny from Siem Reap sitting in front of me again! Congratulations on what you've achieved here. When I read about it in the papers, I had to come at the first opportunity. Your cooking class is causing quite a stir and everything seems to be going swimmingly!'

Munny could only nod. The joy of seeing Dang again still sat like a big lump in his throat.

'How did you get here? Good heavens, I've been looking everywhere for you. I thought Damon had killed you. Man, he was furious! I thought he was going to go for my throat as well. You must have stocked up on everything you needed from his apartment, yes? His money and his stash? Boy, he was seriously not in a good mood!'

Munny nodded. His face showed pain. 'Yes, those were bad times – right in the middle of my breakdown.' He told Dang his harrowing story, leaving out no detail or opportunity for self-criticism. 'I violated almost all five of Buddhism's moral precepts. I took drugs, stole, fooled around with random women, lied, and lost all control over my speech and my senses. I still feel so guilty.'

Dang shook his head repeatedly, in shock. 'Man, if it hadn't been for the mission, you'd probably just be a skeleton somewhere in the outback now, eh?'

Munny nodded his head. 'Yeah, for sure. But Dang, tell me, how are you, Liam and Nicole? Are you still working in Sydney?'

He had so many questions – and finally here were answers! His head was spinning. The thin chirping of crickets in the garden had swelled to an intensity in his ears that was almost painful.

'Well, Liam and Nicole had twins recently – two girls. Poor Liam, he'll have to hold his own in a household full of women now. But Nicole is tough and always brings him back down to earth. Guess what, they named their first daughter Maryam.'

A paralysing pain shot through Munny, ending like a sharp needle in his heart. Silent and with glassy eyes, he nodded.

'When you dropped out at the hotel, Liam had to see how he could replace you. Who do you think joined us?'

Munny shrugged.

'He got Finn over from Siem Reap. It wasn't easy. They didn't really want to let him go. But he was really homesick for Sydney anyway. He felt very comfortable in his new job from the start and fits in well – hey, and he can surf too. Liam and Finn, the two of them, they're a great team!' Dang rolled his eyes.

'It was good for Liam. He didn't have an easy time without you, and he had to deal with quite a few questions about you and your whereabouts. It was as if you had disappeared from the face of the earth,' Dang groaned.

Munny was breathing heavily. 'Dang, I can't tell you how sorry I am for the way I treated you. But you know, the thing with Maryam and Estelle just threw me off the rails. In retrospect, to be honest, I can't really understand what happened to me. I guess I was just a complete idiot who threw all my friends' good advice to the wind. I was blind with pain, Dang! I had never gone through anything so devastating in my life. It was like someone was ripping my heart out, you know?'

Munny swallowed hard. It was the first time he had spoken about his loss. Goosebumps crept over his entire body.

Dang nodded with visible sympathy. His face was a mirror of his soul. Embarrassed, he wiped his eyes.

They sat in silence.

'Hey, Dang, tell me, what are you doing now?'

Dang smiled with satisfaction. 'Liam has made me the chief organiser of all restaurants and events, with Jason's approval. Jason's still the manager of the hotel. I still work in the kitchen with Liam and Finn, but I now have a small office as well where I coordinate everything, half a day at a time on two or three days of the week. I would never have believed that it would be so much fun. But it's exhausting as well and can be a real challenge.'

Munny listened to his friend with fascination. It was good to hear that Dang had been able to give free rein to his energy and initiative.

A trainee chef suddenly put his arm around Munny's shoulder and cleared his throat. 'We're finished for now. Do you still need us?'

Munny looked up at him and smiled. 'No, you've been great today, it's all gone well. Good work! Take some time off and get yourselves something to eat and drink.'

The apprentice gave Munny a nudge. 'Of course! You won't get much out of us otherwise ...' He gave Munny a knowing wink and went back to his group at the adjoining table.

Dang looked at Munny. 'You seem to have found your new family here.'

'Yes, that's right. They've given me so much support from the very beginning, and now I'm giving something back to them. Most of the children have no parents, no home and no one to take care of them. For them, this is family. And since they've been coming to my cooking class, they've really blossomed and come out of their shells. It's like it was for us back then – they're plunging into the wonderful world of tastes and flavours, it gives them motivation.'

Dang shook his head thoughtfully. 'Sometimes it's incredible what life does to us, hmm?' He shot Munny a questioning glance.

'Yes, you're right there – but it's amazing how it fits in with the doctrine of the eternal circle that always closes again. I seem to have come full circle, back to where I once started and where Voramay took me under her wing. Now I take these children under mine.'

'It suits you too, Munny. You play the role of a mentor well, my friend. Tell me, does your restaurant have a name?'

Munny shook his head, a bit stumped. 'No, to be honest, I've never thought about it. You're right. Can you think of something suitable?'

'Why don't you call it "Haven", like Paul with his oasis in Siem Reap?' suggested Dang.

'Well, that would be pinching his idea ... But what do you think of "Heaven on Earth"? For the children here, it is something of a little heaven on earth,' mused Munny.

Dang nodded. 'Yes, that sounds good, and it fits your life well, because you have created and rebuilt your "heaven" yourself.' He scratched the back of his head a little awkwardly. 'Tell me, when was the last time you had contact with your parents?' Munny bit his lip. His guilty conscience had been haunting him for a long time. During his breakdown, he had completely banished them from his mind out of shame. Now he was really afraid of confronting them with what had become of him.

Dang seemed to see his uncertainty. 'Munny, they know about Maryam and Estelle's death. I had to call them because you'd disappeared. They were very shocked by the news. But they were even more worried about you because it was so unlike you just to disappear. I was very sad myself that I couldn't tell them anything. It made them even more desperate. I promised them that if I found you, I would ask you to get in touch with them. Here's their number, in case you don't have it.' Dang handed him a piece of paper with an address and number, along with his own business card bearing the hotel's logo. Apparently, Munny's parents had moved closer to the city.

Munny nodded sheepishly. 'Yes, I know. You're right, but it's so damned hard to make the first move. I need to be able to look them in the eye. I don't know if I can do that.'

'How about you taking a holiday sometime? I could come with you.'

'Yes, that would be good, but I still have to warn my parents and ... call them.' Munny's voice faltered.

'Hey man, you can do this, I'm sure you can. Anyway, I'll have to be on my way presently. Got to be back in Sydney tomorrow afternoon. I'm driving half the distance today and the rest tomorrow.'

Munny looked at the clock. 'Dang, stay a few more minutes. Mel's shift ends soon. She works here as a doctor. I'd like you to meet her. If it weren't for her, I wouldn't have found the energy to do all this.'

Dang raised his eyebrows in astonishment. 'Wow, you really have found your way back to life.'

'Yes, we've been a couple for almost nine months. You'll like her.'

Dang caught his breath. 'Gosh, I almost forgot. Here, this is for you. You left it when you went off in such a mess.' He pulled a rectangular object out of his backpack, wrapped in a dark plastic film. 'Here, maybe you still recognise it.'

Munny gasped. Speechless, he took the plastic wrapping like a raw egg and looked at Dang inquiringly.

'My goodness, I don't believe it, it's my old Khmer book about Cambodian cuisine. I've missed it so much. Where did you find it?' He looked at Dang in disbelief.

'When we had to clear out your apartment, Liam kindly got me to help. I knew how much that book meant to you. After all, that was the beginning of everything, wasn't it?'

Munny nodded, moved. He was incapable of saying anything. He felt as if Voramay were giving him a sign – as if she wanted to tell him, through the book, 'I never gave up on you, not for a moment'.

He embraced Dang and held him close. 'Thank you, thank you so much for your loyal friendship over all these years.'

'I found something else for you in our hotel kitchen. Thought I'd take it with me right away before someone else snapped it up. Here!' Dang held out a narrow rectangular object wrapped in a cloth.

Munny inhaled sharply and audibly as he felt the object and stared at Dang. 'My God, is that what I think it is?'

Dang nodded mysteriously.

Munny's eyes lit up as a small black box with red Japanese characters appeared from under the cloth. 'Paul's knives!' He dropped his jaw. 'Dang, you've given me back my two most valuable possessions. Man, I just can't believe it. I was such an idiot to leave everything behind.'

Dang grinned. 'At last I hear some sensible self-criticism from you. No problem, pal. You see, some things just keep coming back.'

Dang looked at his watch. 'Oh Munny, and there's something else.' He shifted awkwardly, his face serious.

'What?' Munny looked at his friend questioningly. 'Come on, what is it?'

Dang fumbled clumsily in the front pocket of his small backpack, from which he had previously extracted the book. 'Here!' He pulled out an opened envelope, already slightly yellowed and creased.

Munny felt a heatwave surge through his body. Inside was another envelope, addressed to him, sealed. He immediately recognised Voramay's delicate handwriting.

'But ... how?' Munny looked at Dang in amazement.

Dang nodded. 'Yes, it was all a bit bizarre. When you disappeared and I had to call your parents about Maryam ...' he faltered. ' ...we talked for a long time. Somehow it was good for both sides, for them and me, to talk about it. I didn't actually have anyone I could really talk to. They cried a lot ... so did I.' Dang wiped the back of his hand over his eyes. Munny, eyes glazed over, put an arm around his shoulder.

'You won't believe how much they missed you during the time you were working in Sydney. But they didn't want to let you see it, because they were afraid you would quit your job and come back because of them. Voramay was a great support to them. When she sensed that she didn't have much time left, she confided in your parents. That was shortly after your wedding ceremony. You and Maryam had just left ...'

Munny wrinkled his brow. 'She "confided in them"? What do you mean by that?'

'Well ... Voramay told them a long-kept secret. About you!'

Every tendon in Munny's body was tense as a guitar string. He stared at Dang in disbelief.

'Apparently she knew more than she let on about your background. But out of consideration for you and your foster-parents, she never mentioned it. She didn't want to bring more trouble into your life.'

'Tell me, is it something bad? What are you saying? Have my parents told you something about my background? Is Kongsita my real father after all?' Munny could no longer contain his impatience.

'It's about your biological parents. Voramay told Arun and Chenda everything on her deathbed. They told me that it was very hard for them to bear. But Munny, they gave me the feeling that they had never lost hope of seeing you again.'

Dang gave Munny the yellowing paper from the open envelope. It had the logo of a Siem Reap writing office at the top. Munny read the first lines on the yellow paper.

'Dear Mr Munny, I am writing to you on behalf of your parents, Arun and Chenda ...' At that moment it dawned on him that his parents, who had never learned to write, must have visited this office to have the letter written to Dang and him.

Dear Munny, we miss you so much. Our thoughts are with you wherever you are. Although Dang told us that you left the hotel, we hope that your good karma has remained with you ...

He guessed that Dang had spared them the degrading details in his narrative, just telling them that he had gone away.

... as you know, Voramay has passed into the eternal wheel of life. Before her passing, she summoned us to the monastery to ask us for a few small things for her cremation ceremony, which we were very happy to do for her. But she also wanted to confide in us what she called her 'life's secret'. At first, her words came as a great shock to us. But she explained that it was the will of fate. 'Nothing happens for no reason,' she said. She wanted you to learn about it through this letter, which she had written long before her death. We are enclosing her letter with this one.

Please get in touch when you can find time. We miss you so much. Your Arun and Chenda ...

Tears of emotion ran down Munny's cheeks, and dripped onto the paper. Normally, children don't address their parents by their first names. That's what decency and respect between parents and children demands. But his parents had signed with their first names. That showed Munny only too clearly how much they cared about him and missed him.

Dang looked him in the eye. 'I'm so glad I found you again, I really am! I missed you so much. And now I can finally give you the letter from Voramay. It's a great weight off my shoulders. You'd better find a quiet moment to read it.'

Munny nodded, unable to utter a sound. Dang gave him a shake. 'I don't want to be nosy, but let me know sooner rather than later what the letter says about your origins. Maybe your biological father's name is Bocuse.' Laughing loudly, he slapped his hands on his thighs. 'Man, if that's so, I'd join your team any day of the week!'

Munny grinned at Dang's pretended naivety, and then lapsed into a thoughtful silence. 'Dang, you know what, we'll read it together. That would help me to cope.' He took a deep breath and carefully, almost tenderly, opened the envelope. He looked meaningfully at Dang as he did so. Voramay's delicate handwriting appeared on the carefully folded paper.

Munny, son of my heart,

You know, from the very first minute you were found by Kongsita, our destinies were intertwined. Our journey together began way back, before we were ever aware of it.

The truth about your life was first revealed to me in the ancient temple walls of the Preah Khan temple, 'my temple' as I called it – even if I wasn't conscious of it at the time.

The day after Kongsita found you, I went there early in the morning. I prayed for good karma for you and that you would find a good family. Without having even set eyes on you, I knew that you had to be a strong character, given the adverse circumstances in which you were found. And as it turned out, you really were a strong-willed, ambitious and extraordinary boy.

Munny looked up from the letter. He could see Voramay smiling at those words.

She was so present at that moment, he could literally feel her. Goosebumps ran over his body.

Late that afternoon, one of the park rangers, Nu, came to see me and told me about a young man living locally who had asked him about me and my monastery. He knew this young man. His family could evidently afford to send him to college to learn English. He apparently earned his college tuition by becoming a certified guide for the Angkor Wat temple complex. Nu said the boy was a very decent person.

I had almost forgotten this conversation when, many days later, a young man came to see me in the library of our monastery. His name was Sam. I immediately recognised his face with its slightly foreign features. He was one of the guides who showed tourists around the temples. He told me that he was the son of an Englishman and a Cambodian woman, had a small silk business in the city, and was preparing for his studies in England.

I asked him if we had not already met at the Preah Khan temple. He honestly confirmed what I already knew. He was very agitated, almost distraught, and didn't quite know how to express himself. Something seemed to be weighing heavily on his mind. He asked if I remembered the day he came to me at the temple with a young female tourist. I remembered it very well. In particular, I remembered the sad eyes of a young European woman.

The poor boy could hardly contain his excitement. He asked me why I had assured the young woman back then so emphatically that everything is good for something and nothing happens in vain. I was amazed that he remembered my words so well. He cried and said that they had both felt that I was telling them about bad karma.

In tears, he confessed that the tourist had been his girlfriend for two years. Her name was Ines and she was from Spain. She visited him regularly, and nine months ago she moved to Siem Reap for a planned break to be with him. Of course, she stayed in a small hostel because he could not have taken her home. They kept their relationship secret.

Apparently, Ines had returned to the city in tears after visiting me at the temple and had wanted to leave that same day. She could not

222

be persuaded by Sam to stay. In a letter, she told him that she was so sorry for all of this and that she had made a huge mistake. He should forgive her. She did not want to stand in the way of his studies.

I guessed that they were both in their early to mid-twenties.

I thought I had to comfort the boy for his broken heart. It turned out differently.

Dang looked at Munny, confused. 'What's that got to do with you?'

Munny shook his head, baffled. But he had a vague inkling that made his scalp tingle.

In tears, the poor lad made a terrible confession to me. He was at a loss and couldn't talk to anyone about it. It was a great burden on him.

When Ines came to him back then, they thought they would have a rosy future together. He in England, she in Spain – only a short distance apart. They were looking forward to it so much, and made plans.

Their plans were painfully thwarted.

Ines became pregnant. She realised it quite late. Sam described to me the panic that took hold of them both at the time. All their plans were gone like a puff of smoke. Her visit here, initially planned for three months, became nine months. Sam had already made up his mind to tell his parents everything but Ines stopped him. She wanted to bring the child into the world alone and flew to Phnom Penh to give birth. Sam begged her to come back to Siem Reap. Ines gave in to his pleas and came back with their child.

During this time they were both in turmoil, arguing a lot and feeling very unhappy. Ines wanted to go back to Spain, but without the child. She was gripped by her fears, and talked about having to give the child up for adoption. Sam tried to learn the reasons for her panic and for her choice of such a drastic solution. But she closed herself off from him even more. During the adoption formalities, they then realised that they would have to provide a lot of information about themselves and their background. This scared them both off, especially Ines.

One day later, in the early evening, they met at Ines' hostel.

She arrived drenched in the rain and out of breath. She did not have the child. Sam wanted to know where the baby was. She calmed him down by saying that she had left it anonymously at a monastery. She didn't tell him which one. Sam was beside himself. They argued and shouted at each other.

Sam cried uncontrollably in front of me as he told me this.

He was able to persuade her to go to a temple the day before she left and ask for forgiveness, in hope that this bad karma would not catch up with her.

So these two people crossed my path just one day after you were found by the side of the road in the middle of the rainy season. Sam and Ines were standing in front of me asking for forgiveness as I was looking for a new family for you.

Samsara – how the circle closes again!

I wondered whether I should tell Kongsita the truth. Or later, tell Chenda and Arun. After much prayer and reflection, I decided against it, so as not to pre-empt your personal decision about knowing who your biological parents were. I knew I didn't have the right to do that.

Please understand that I refrained out of respect for those generous people, your foster-parents and Kongsita and his wife. Your path seemed to be laid out, your place was here, and my karma had assigned me a specific role in it.

In order not to hurt Sam even more in his certainty of having made a big mistake, I never told him what I knew – that you had been found on the roadside and who your new parents were.

Sam went to England. He always came to see me when he visited his parents here. He contacted Ines again in Europe and tried to find out what had become of her. She wrote him a short message saying that her life was back on track and congratulating him on his graduation. They never met again.

Munny, I know that this letter about your origins will stir you up quite a bit, but just remember what we believe in. It is not important where we come from or who we are. Only our actions and thoughts speak.

On the small piece of paper enclosed, you will find Sam's address. Please use this knowledge mindfully and patiently. Think carefully. Always remember what I told you: to listen to your gut feeling.

Sometimes it's better not to dwell on the past or dream of the future. Just focus on the present moment and act accordingly. We are all the result of our thoughts.

Dear son of my heart, I would like to give you something for your journey through life – an inner awareness of one thing:

that when I set out on my path into samsara, wherever you may be, I am there too. Never stop believing in that!

Your Voramay

Munny gave his tears free rein, wiping them away again and again with embarrassment.

Dang put a hand on his shoulder and shook his head in disbelief. 'Wow, so then you're practically half European.'

'Well, apparently not just half. A little more, actually. Man, I've got to digest that first.' He shook his head in disbelief.

Dang looked at him questioningly. 'What are you going to do now?'

'I don't know, I think I need to let it all sink in.' Munny was stunned. He felt like an extra in a film. A film where an episode suddenly changes from black and white to full colour. A whole new perspective.

'Yes, you do that,' Dang said, rousing him from his confused thoughts.

'I think Voramay is right when she tells you to proceed with caution. Take your time. Maybe you can find enough answers from your parents ... er, foster-parents in Siem Reap. Talk to them about it. I think they need your support now.'

'Yes, you're right, I have to go to Cambodia first.'

Munny smiled at his friend of many years. Dang looked visibly relieved. He felt just the same way.

'Hello, gorgeous.' Mel approached him from behind.

'Dang! This is my Mel,' Munny exclaimed happily. 'I'm so glad you two have time to meet before Dang has to get back to Sydney.'

Dang held out his hand to Mel, but she opened her arms. The two embraced.

Munny couldn't help smiling. Mel must have recognised who the visitor was immediately.

They talked for a while, laughing freely. Dang dug up stories from his and Munny's shared past for Mel's benefit. He was still the same joker he had been in the old days.

'But now I really should go,' Dang said at last. 'It's back to work for me – tomorrow at the latest.' He rose and hugged Mel briefly, then gave Munny such a massive hug that it almost took his breath away.

When Dang had left and they were alone in the garden again, Mel and Munny sat down on their swing.

'That's a nice, sympathetic friend of yours. I like him. He's so direct and has such an open face.'

Munny nodded, lost in thought. Yes, he was really incredibly lucky to have such a good friend.

'Mel, could you imagine going to Siem Reap with me next month to visit my parents? Because of the mess I was in, I haven't contacted them in ages. I want to make up for it. They've done so much for me. Dang would probably come too. Actually it was his idea.'

Mel smiled and looked Munny in the eye. 'I'd like to meet your parents.' She kissed him tenderly on the lips.

They looked in the half-darkness of the garden at a group of youngsters laughing as they told each other about their misadventures in cooking school.

They couldn't help but laugh with them.

Munny thought of his wise old mentor. In talking to Dang, he'd realised how right she had been in saying that you have to learn from your misfortunes.

'Those who want something find ways; those who don't, find reasons.'

CHARACTERS IN THE BOOK

Munny	the foundling (Cambodian 'intelligent')
Arun	Foster-father of Munny (Cambodian 'morning sun')
Chenda	Foster-mother of Munny (Cambodian 'wisdom')
Vanna	Mother of Chenda, has a soup kitchen (Cambodian 'gold')
Kongsita	Tuk-tuk driver
Tevi	Wife of Kongsita (Cambodian 'angel')
Sopheap	Daughter of Kongsita (Cambodian 'friendly')
Voramay	Buddhist nun, Munny's mentor
Kunthea	Midwife (Cambodian 'sweet-smelling')
Boran	School friend of Munny's (Cambodian 'very old')
Paul and Sara	Swiss head chef and his partner, founders of the Haven restaurant in Siem Reap
Maryam	Munny's wife, Eurasian, Malaysian
Dang	Friend of Munny's during his professional training, Cambodian Vietnamese
Luc	Chef at Raffles Grand Hotel, French
Finn	Sous-chef at Raffles, Australian, a friend of Paul's
Ethan	CEO and Managing Director of Raffles, Irish

Liam	Chef de cuisine, Sydney
Nicole	Wife of Liam, English, grew up in Australia
Jason	CEO and Managing Director of partner hotel in Sydney
Damon	Drug dealer, Australian
Thérèse	Head of Mission Australia, French
Mel	Assistant doctor at Mission Australia, English
Sunny (Sunan)	Friend of Munny's at Mission Australia, Canadian-Thai
Haven	Restaurant with cooking class run by Paul
Heaven on Earth	Munny's cookery school

ABOUT THIS BOOK

After more than 30 years of travelling across Southeast Asia, Siem Reap has become a real place of power for me. During my regular visits there, I have built up a wonderful little circle of friends. This mystical place has an inspiring effect and triggers something fascinating and special for each visitor in his or her own way.

The book and Munny's life story are biographical, and are based on the life of a person I am friends with who still lives in Siem Reap and Phnom Penh.

The characters of Kongsita, Paul and Sara and Voramay also actually exist and are part of my little circle. My elderly nun sadly passed away during Covid times. I miss her very much. She gave me insights into the Buddhist way of reasoning. A method of argumentation that can be very useful in our industrialised world as well – especially in mediating between opposite poles and divergent points of view, based on the art of getting people around the table and working out solutions together.

The life stories of my characters are interwoven with other tales that people from Siem Reap and the surrounding area have told me about their lives, all coming together to form a work of fiction.

I am grateful that I was able to be part of all this and still am a part of it today.

My special thanks are owing to Paul and Sara with their restaurant and training centre the 'Haven'.

It is a project that involves a lot of heart and soul. Had it not been for them, many of their young trainees would still be working in the rice fields without ever having attended school. The Haven is a place where the students are given an incentive to make something of themselves, by working with discipline and a lot of ambition. There are many more opportunities open to them after their training than before.

A good friend of mine, Sampoan, who comes from a family of seven children, has managed to become self-employed thanks to school education. Her father, a professor of physics and maths at a local secondary school, had to supplement his meagre salary by giving guided tours to bird-watching tourists – birds are his main hobby – in order to feed his large family.

Sampoan has inherited the same enthusiasm from him, the only one of the seven children to do so. I first met her on a tour through the jungle outside Siem Reap. She has since come up with a bright idea, owing something to her own ingenuity and something to her schooling, as well as to the boom in hotel building in Siem Reap – to collect kitchen waste from hotels, and turn it into good humus. Soil that is urgently needed for urban parks, green spaces and new gardens in hotels. A win-win situation for both sides.

As a result she has become a successful businesswoman and is now able to support her parents.

The book is an inspiration for individual trippers and global travellers, inviting them to experience these places of many stories with an open mind and with their very own imagination, and to compare the two contrasting worlds of Cambodia and Australia.

Two worlds which could hardly be more different from one another – from the over two-thousand-year-old world of the Khmer, with the Buddhist-influenced attitude to life that has prevailed since the 12th century, to the New World of Australia, which can still be described as very young and almost experimentally diverse in its way of life. The prevailing attitude there has a sporty, relaxed approach, characteristic of the typical Australian philosophy, the 'Australian way of life'.

But one thing above all connects these two worlds – the love of nature.

THE AUTHOR

born in southern Germany in 1963, spent part of his childhood in the south of France. He grew up speaking three languages. His passion for travelling off the beaten track was ignited early in his youth. The author has been touring Southeast Asia for more than thirty years.

He has been drawn to travelled to Siem Reap and Singapore for almost twenty years. Over the years, he collected very personal life stories from his friends there, which inspired him to write this novel. With it, he wants to inspire travelling enthusiasts and bring them closer to these mystical places. The debut novel 'Munny', written under the pseudonym Flynn Dubois by Elke Wittmann, is the first part of a fascinating life story.

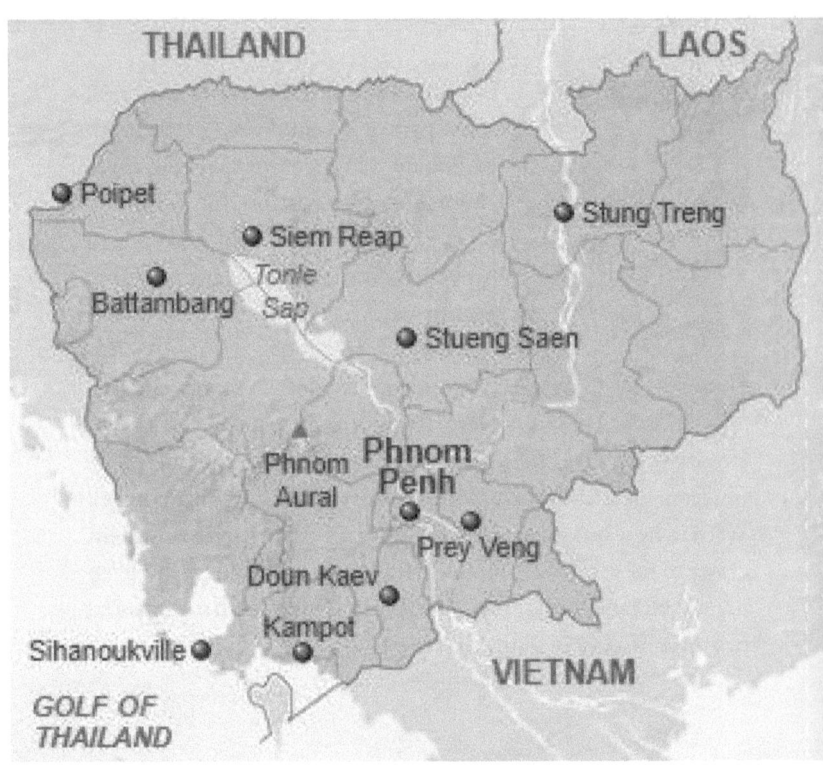

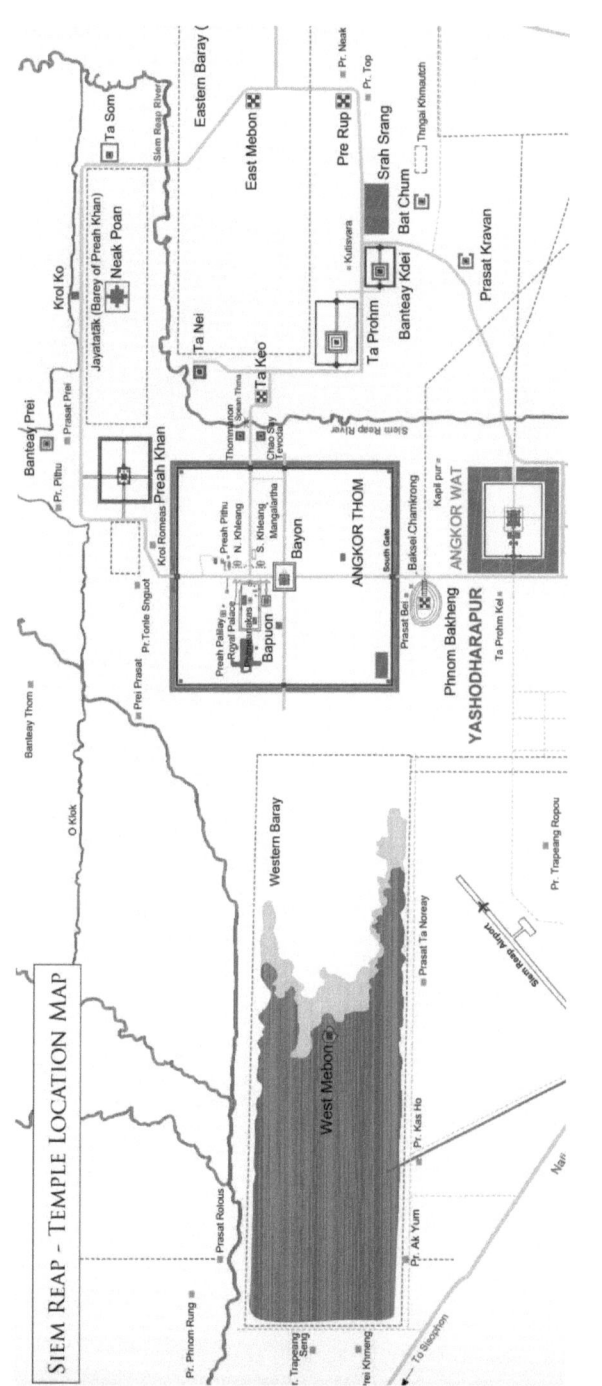

SIEM REAP – TEMPLE LOCATION MAP